"Brenda Jackson writes romance that sizzles
and characters you fall in love with."
—*New York Times* and *USA TODAY*
bestselling author Lori Foster

"Jackson's trademark ability to weave
multiple characters and side stories together
makes shocking truths all the more exciting."
—*Publishers Weekly*

"There is no getting away from the sex appeal
and charm of Jackson's Westmoreland family."
—*RT Book Reviews* on *Feeling the Heat*

"Jackson's characters are wonderful, strong,
colorful and hot enough to burn the pages."
—*RT Book Reviews* on *Westmoreland's Way*

"The kind of sizzling, heart-tugging story
Brenda Jackson is famous for."
—*RT Book Reviews* on *Spencer's Forbidden Passion*

"This is entertainment at its best."
—*RT Book Reviews* on *Star of His Heart*

Praise for

Dear Reader,

I love writing about the Westmorelands because they exemplify what a strong family is all about, mainly the sharing of love and support. For that reason, when I was given the chance to present them in a trilogy, I was excited and ready to dive into the lives of Zane, Canyon and Stern Westmoreland.

It is hard to believe that Zane is my twenty-fourth Westmoreland novel. It seemed like it was only yesterday when I introduced you to Delaney and her five brothers. I knew by the time I wrote Thorn's story that I just had to tell you about their cousins that were spread out over Montana, Texas, California and Colorado.

It has been an adventure and I enjoyed sharing it with you. I've gotten your emails and snail mails letting me know how much you adore those Westmoreland men, and I appreciate hearing from you. Each Westmoreland—male or female—is unique and the way love conquers their hearts is heartwarming, breathtaking and totally satisfying.

In this story, Zane, who is considered an expert when it comes to women, discovers that when it comes to his own love life, he needs to rethink some of his philosophies if he wants to capture the heart of the woman who has captured his.

I hope you enjoy this story about Zane and Channing Hasting.

Happy reading!

Brenda Jackson

BRENDA JACKSON

Zane

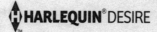

To my husband, the love of my life and my best friend,
Gerald Jackson, Sr.

To everyone who enjoys reading about the Westmoreland family,
this one is for you!

Happy is the man that findeth wisdom,
and the man that getteth understanding.
—*Proverbs* 3:13

ISBN-13: 978-0-373-73252-4

THE WESTMORELANDS: ZANE

Copyright © 2013 by Brenda Streater Jackson

PLEASE RECYCLE
THIS PRODUCT IS RECYCLABLE

Recycling programs
for this product may
not exist in your area.

Printed in U.S.A.

HARLEQUIN®
™ www.Harlequin.com

BRENDA JACKSON

is a die "heart" romantic who married her childhood sweetheart and still proudly wears the "going steady" ring he gave her when she was fifteen. Because she believes in the power of love, Brenda's stories always have happy endings. In her real-life love story, Brenda and her husband of more than forty years live in Jacksonville, Florida, and have two sons.

A *New York Times* bestselling author of more than seventy-five romance titles, Brenda is a recent retiree who now divides her time between family, writing and traveling with Gerald. You may write Brenda at P.O. Box 28267, Jacksonville, Florida 32226, by email at WriterBJackson@aol.com or visit her website at www.brendajackson.net.

THE DENVER WESTMORELAND FAMILY TREE

Raphel and Gemma Westmoreland

Stern Westmoreland (Paula Bailey)

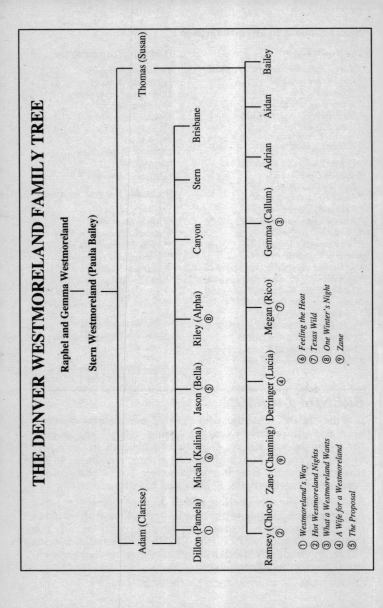

Thomas (Susan)

Adam (Clarisse)

Dillon (Pamela) ①   Micah (Kalina) ⑥   Jason (Bella) ⑤   Riley (Alpha) ⑧   Canyon   Stern   Brisbane

Ramsey (Chloe) ②   Zane (Channing) ⑨   Derringer (Lucia) ④   Megan (Rico) ⑦   Gemma (Callum) ③   Adrian   Aidan   Bailey

① *Westmoreland's Way*
② *Hot Westmoreland Nights*
③ *What a Westmoreland Wants*
④ *A Wife for a Westmoreland*
⑤ *The Proposal*

⑥ *Feeling the Heat*
⑦ *Texas Wild*
⑧ *One Winter's Night*
⑨ *Zane*

One

"What do you mean Channing's back in Denver?" Zane Westmoreland dropped down in the chair across from his sister, a dark frown covering his face.

He fixed his gaze on Bailey, waiting on her response. Bailey knew that any mention of Channing Hastings would make him mad, but it seemed she was intent on ignoring him while she continued to eat her bowl of ice cream. Anyone else would have jumped at the anger that was apparent in his voice but not this particular sister. She didn't do anything until she was good and ready. While he waited, even more irritation bubbled up inside of him.

After what seemed like an enormous period of silence, Bailey finally angled her head. "I meant just what I said. I saw Channing today when I had lunch at the hospital with Megan. I understand she arrived in town last week. She looks good by the way."

Zane wasn't surprised. As far as he was concerned, there was never a time when Channing hadn't looked good…even after a sweaty workout session at the gym.

Suddenly, unbridled fury worked its way along his stomach lining. Why should he care how an ex-girlfriend looked? More importantly, why did the thought of her being back in town trigger such deep-seated anger within him?

Zane could answer that question without much thought. It hadn't been their breakup that still pissed him off but rather *how* they had broken up. Usually he was the one who decided when one of his relationships ended, but Channing had surprised the hell out of him and ended it herself.

"Is Channing's fiancé with her?" He could have bitten off his tongue for asking.

"No, she's only here for six weeks, hosting a medical symposium at the hospital." Bailey didn't say anything for a minute and then, "That man got under my skin."

Zane lifted a brow. "What man?"

"Channing's fiancé. He was checking out the women at Megan's wedding reception, even with Channing standing right beside him. He had a lot of nerve."

Zane had noticed the man's roving eyes, as well. He really shouldn't care. If Channing was inclined to put up with that kind of foolishness, that was her business. It shouldn't concern him. But it did.

He glanced out the window while his mind wandered back in time. He had dated Channing longer than he'd dated any other woman—nine months exactly. Things had been almost perfect between them. But then she'd started hinting that she wanted more from their relationship. That was when he'd reiterated that he was not the marrying kind and never intended to be.

She never brought up the issue again, and Zane had assumed things were back to normal. But less than a month later, out of the clear blue sky, she told him that she had accepted a job at a hospital in Atlanta and would be moving away.

That had annoyed the hell out of him. She was trying to force his hand, and he wouldn't allow any woman to do that. So he'd called her bluff, refusing to offer a proposal. But then she'd moved to Atlanta as planned. That was almost two years ago, and he hadn't seen or heard from her until she'd shown up at his sister's wedding last month an engaged woman.

Engaged.

The very thought made him angry. She'd had the nerve to bring her fiancé to the wedding knowing full well Zane would be there. And like Bailey had said, the man had checked out other women even with Channing by his side. That she was so desperate to have a ring on her finger that she would settle for such a man—the realization made Zane madder.

"This is simply delicious."

Bailey's words intruded on his thoughts. He glanced over at his sister, and his frown deepened. He had come home to find her sitting at his kitchen table like she lived there. In his current mood, her presence aggravated him. "And what do you think you're doing?"

She smiled. "What does it look like? I'm eating ice cream."

"*My* ice cream," he muttered. "How did you get in here, anyway? I changed the locks on my door."

Bailey leaned back in her chair and chuckled. "I noticed. Did you forget that I know how to pick a lock, Zane? Bane taught me ages ago. And as far as the ice cream, you only bought it because you knew I'd eat it.

You don't even like ice cream, and this is one of my favorite flavors."

"They're all your favorite flavors," he said, forcing himself not to grin. The last thing he needed was for her to think he was getting soft. And as far as picking locks, he had forgotten that talent had been just one of the many ways she and their cousin Bane used to get into trouble.

Getting up from the table, he headed for the door.

"Hey, where are you going?" Bailey called after him.

"Since I can't find peace in my own home, I'm going to ride my horse a spell. I'll be gone for an hour or so and hopefully that will give you time to find someone else to visit."

He then walked out the door and slammed it shut behind him.

"Channing, wait up!"

Channing stopped and turned around. She smiled when she saw Megan Claiborne walking briskly toward her. Megan had been one of the first doctors she'd become good friends with while working at the hospital four years ago, and their friendship had remained intact. Last month, Megan married Rico Claiborne, a gorgeous Bradley Cooper look-alike who worked as a private investigator in Philly. To divide their time between Philadelphia and Denver, Megan worked six months as a doctor of anesthesiology in Denver and the other six months at a hospital in Philly.

Megan looked different. "Marriage agrees with you," Channing said when Megan came to a stop in front of her.

Her comment made an infectious smile settle on Megan's lips. "You think so?"

"I know so. There's a radiant glow about you. You seem happy. I mean truly happy," Channing said.

Megan's smile widened. "I *am* happy, and I have to concur that marriage does agree with me. Rico is the best. He's everything I could ever want in a man."

"Then you have a reason to smile and look radiant." Channing was happy for her friend and she wanted that same happiness and radiance for herself.

Long marriages were common in Channing's family. Her parents had been married for more than thirty-five years, and her grandparents would be celebrating their sixtieth wedding anniversary next year. Her aunts and uncles had been in wedded bliss for more than twenty years, and her cousins and oldest brother, Juan, had all been married eight years or more.

When Channing had dated Megan's brother Zane a few years back, she had believed he was the one. Although he had told her more than once that he never intended to marry, she'd actually thought he'd change his mind. Over the course of their relationship, although he'd never spoken any words of love, his actions had convinced her he had feelings for her. He'd been so attentive, possessive and protective. She was the first woman he'd invited to his family's weekly dinner gatherings and the first woman he'd given a key to his place. So, quite naturally, she had assumed she meant more to him than all the women he'd dated in the past.

But as time went by, it became obvious that he had no intention of making their relationship more than the affair that it was. Then, one day after they'd dated exclusively for almost nine months—she'd come out and asked him how she saw their relationship evolving. He'd told her nothing had changed. He never intended to marry. He'd said that although he cared for her, he didn't love her—and never would.

She'd appreciated his honesty, but his words had hurt. To protect her heart from further damage, she'd decided to move on. She wanted more.

A week later, she'd accepted the position as a neurologist at Emory Hospital in Atlanta. She didn't tell Zane about her plans until the week before she was ready to leave Denver. She knew Zane was still angry with her about the way she'd ended things, but it wasn't as if she'd left town without telling him.

"I wanted to ask you to come to my family's Friday night chow-down," Megan said, intruding into Channing's thoughts.

Channing winced. "You know I can't do that."

"Why not? Things between you and Zane didn't work out, and you moved on. As far as I'm concerned, it was my brother's loss."

"But I don't want to make things uncomfortable, Megan. I saw the way Zane was staring me down at your wedding. He didn't like the way I ended things between us."

"Forget Zane." Megan bristled. "Did he honestly expect things to continue between the two of you without him ever making a serious commitment?"

Channing shrugged, even though she knew Zane *had* expected that. They had been dating exclusively, and to him that was enough. "I guess he did," Channing said softly, remembering how hard it had been to leave him, to move forward and not look back.

"Well, it served him right to find out he was wrong." Megan took a moment and seemed to choose her next words carefully. "Channing, you were my friend long before you became involved with Zane. You moved away, and now you're back for a short time. There's nothing wrong with me inviting you to dine with my family."

Channing could see plenty wrong with it. "Thanks, but I think it's best if I don't accept your invitation. I'll be in Denver for at least three weeks, six weeks if I decide to do a second symposium. Considering how Zane feels about me, he and I should keep our distance."

Megan didn't push...at least not right now. Channing knew her friend wouldn't let it drop. "You're welcome to come. If you change your mind, let me know."

Channing nodded, but she wouldn't be changing her mind.

By the time Zane had returned home, Bailey was gone. He headed up the stairs to shower, refusing to admit he missed his sister already. She was known for her drop-in visits not only to him but also to her other brothers, sisters and cousins.

Presently, there were fifteen Denver Westmorelands. His parents had had eight children: five boys—Ramsey, Zane, Derringer and the twins, Aiden and Adrian—and three girls—Megan, Gemma and Bailey. Uncle Adam and Aunt Clarisse had had seven sons: Dillon, Micah, Jason, Riley, Canyon, Stern and Brisbane. Over the past few years, nearly everyone had gotten married. Megan had married last month, and Riley would marry in September. The only holdouts were him, the twins, Bailey, Canyon, Stern and Bane.

His parents and uncle and aunt had died in a plane crash nearly twenty years ago, leaving Zane's brother Ramsey and his cousin Dillon in charge of the family. It hadn't been easy, especially since several of their siblings and cousins had been under the age of sixteen. Together, Dillon and Ramsey had worked hard and made sacrifices to keep the Westmorelands together. When the state of Colorado tried forcing Dillon to put the youngest four in foster homes, he had refused.

The deaths had been the hardest on those youngest four—the twins, Aiden and Adrian, and Brisbane and Bailey. Everyone had known that their acts of rebellion were their way of handling the grief of losing their parents. Now, the twins had finished college and were working in their chosen professions: Aiden as a doctor and Adrian as an engineer. Brisbane was in the navy and Bailey…was still Bailey. Considered the baby of the family, at twenty-six she worked for *Simply Irresistible,* a magazine for today's up-and-coming woman that was owned by Ramsey's wife, Chloe. But even with a full-time job, Bailey still managed to remind everyone she could be a force to reckon with when she put her mind to it.

When Zane reached his bedroom, he glanced out the window at the acres and acres of land surrounding him. Westmoreland Country. Since Dillon was the oldest, he had inherited the main house along with the three hundred acres it sat on. Everyone else, upon reaching the age of twenty-five, received one hundred acres to call their own. Thanks to Bailey's creative mind, each of their spreads were given names—Ramsey's Web, Zane's Hideout, Derringer's Dungeon, Megan's Meadows, Gemma's Gem, Jason's Place, Stern's Stronghold and Canyon's Bluff. It was beautiful land that encompassed mountains, valleys, lakes, rivers and streams.

Zane loved his home, a two-story structure with a wraparound porch. He had more than enough space for himself and a family—if he ever chose to marry. But since settling down with one woman was not in his plans, he had the place all to himself. Some people did better by themselves, and he was one of those people.

Except when it came to business. He, his brother Derringer and his cousin Jason were partners in a lucrative horse breeding and training business along with several of his Westmoreland cousins who lived in Montana and Texas. The partnership was doing extremely well financially, with horse buyers extending all the way to the Middle East. Ever since one of their horses, Prince Charming, had placed in the Kentucky Derby a few years ago, potential clients had been continually coming out of the woodwork.

He was happy with his work. Zane liked the outdoors. The only thing he liked better was women. He didn't have a problem with the revolving door to his bedroom, and he didn't intend for any woman to get it in her head that she could be the one. There wasn't a woman alive who could make him think about settling down.

A quick flash of pain across his gut let him know he wasn't being truthful about that. There *had* been one woman. Dr. Channing Hastings.

Zane's sister Megan had introduced them, and he had been attracted to Channing from the first time he'd seen her. In addition to her beauty, she had a luscious scent that drew him like a bee to honey. She was the very thing erotic fantasies were made of. He'd only intended to date her for a couple of months. Then, the next thing he knew, he was in an exclusive relationship.

Zane reached under his bed for the locked box he'd placed there. Using the key he kept on his key ring, he opened the box and pulled out the calendar that was inside. It was a personalized photo calendar that Channing had made for him as a gift on his thirty-fifth birthday. Had it been almost two years ago?

He flipped through the calendar, beginning with January. By the time he'd gotten to December, he had worked up a sweat. Seeing Channing dressed in such scanty attire—a different outfit for every month—had sent memories soaring through his mind. In January, she wore a floor-length red gown, the same one she'd worn to a charity benefit he'd taken her to at the hospital and the same one he'd loved taking off of her later that night. By December, she was wearing nothing at all while stretched across her bed in one damn hot position, her body barely covered by a white bedspread decked with colorful Christmas ornaments. She had one of those *I want you now* looks on her face. The photographer had been another female doctor whose hobby was photography, and she had captured Channing in some unbelievable poses. Channing Hastings was definitely a beautiful woman.

She had skin the color of rich mocha, a beautiful pair of hazel eyes, high cheekbones, a perky nose, full lips and a luxurious mane of golden-brown hair. The one constant in each photo was the necklace around her neck. It was the gold one he had given her. The same one she had returned when she'd told him she was leaving Denver.

Reaching into the box, he pulled out that same necklace, remembering the day he'd bought it. He'd been in Montana at a jewelry store with his cousin Durango, who'd wanted to buy a birthday gift for his wife, Savannah. Zane had seen the crescent moon and immediately known he wanted it for Channing. At the time, he had refused to question why, he'd just known that seeing it around her neck was important to him.

After Channing left, he'd flipped through the calendar and pulled out the necklace too many times, which was why he'd given the locked box to Megan for safekeeping. He'd been tired of torturing himself. Although Megan would have been curious about what was inside, he'd trusted her enough to know she would not open the box. He couldn't say the same for Bailey, who, as she'd reminded him today, had a fondness for picking locks. Megan had kept the box for almost a year, but he'd gotten it back from her when she'd taken that trip to Texas with Rico last year.

Megan had invited Channing to the wedding last month, even though he'd asked her not to. However, like Bailey, Megan had a mind of her own and didn't like her brothers telling her what to do. And what teed him off more than the wedding invitation was that he'd been over to Megan's place a few nights ago to welcome the newlyweds back to Denver, and she hadn't mentioned anything about Channing returning to town. He was convinced there was no way she hadn't known.

Zane placed the calendar and necklace back in the box, locked it shut and slid it back under his bed. He then stripped off his clothes to take a shower. His and Channing's paths probably wouldn't cross while she was in town.

But...maybe they should.

It was time he looked at the situation differently, more objectively. He had gotten over Channing months ago, and she had evidently gotten over him. She was an engaged woman. He was happy with his life. She was happy with hers.

He stepped in the shower with his mind made up. He felt rather pleased with the decision and already he considered it done. He would seek out Channing and pay her a visit.

There was nothing wrong with welcoming her back to town.

Two

Channing bent to lower the projector screen when a pair of dark leather boots came into view. The boots were followed by a rich, masculine aroma that she would recognize anytime, anyplace. Her stomach knotted as she slowly straightened.

Her eyes moved up past a pair of jeans-clad thighs, a lean waist, a firm stomach and muscled shoulders. Her gaze unerringly landed on a pair of gorgeous dark brown eyes, creamy chestnut-brown skin, an aquiline nose, sharp cheekbones, full lips and a strong chin.

Zane Westmoreland was almost too handsome to be real. She'd thought that very thing the first time she'd seen him three years ago, right here at this very hospital. He had come to repair his sister's flat tire, and Megan had introduced them. Channing's life hadn't been the same since.

She drew in a long breath and slowly released it. "Zane."

"Channing. I heard you were in town, so I thought I would come by and welcome you back."

Channing leaned against the podium she'd stood behind earlier. There were any number of plausible reasons for Zane to show up at the hospital's lecture hall, but for the life of her, she couldn't think of a valid one. He claimed he wanted to welcome her back to town, but just last month, when she'd seen him at Megan's wedding, he had refused to say a single word to her.

"Thanks, Zane." She could mention that she was only in town for three to six weeks but decided it wasn't any of his business. Two years ago she had left Denver to move on, and she had.

"So, you're still engaged I see," he said when she moved to the desk to place a stack of handouts in her briefcase.

She fought back a scowl. "Is there any reason why I wouldn't be?"

"I guess not."

"And what about you?" Channing asked, crossing her arms over her chest. "I take it you're still eluding serious commitments?"

She noticed the muscle that flicked in his jaw. "If you're asking if I'm still single, with no thoughts of settling down, then the answer is yes. That won't ever change." And without missing a beat, he asked, "Did Mark come with you?"

She frowned. Why was he all up in her business? "My fiancé's name is Mack, and no, he's still in Atlanta."

"He's a banker, right?"

Channing clicked her briefcase closed, wondering why Zane felt it necessary to go over information he already knew. Although he had avoided both her and

Mack at the wedding, Megan had said Zane had questioned her at the wedding reception.

"Yes, Mack's a banker." There was no need to tell him the Hammond family owned several banks that were spread across Georgia, Tennessee and Florida.

She turned to Zane and tried to ignore how totally, utterly male he looked. She felt a deep fluttering in her stomach when her eyes connected to his. He had soft bedroom eyes, eyes that could educate a woman as to what true desire was all about. She, of all people, should know. Yes, some things in her life had changed, but it seemed the charge she got out of seeing Zane Westmoreland hadn't. Why was her body betraying her this way?

"Well, that's it for the day. It was good seeing you again, Zane."

"Same here. I figured sooner or later I'd run into you at one of those Westmoreland family dinners. I thought we should clear the air now so neither of us would feel uncomfortable."

So that's what this little visit was about? Channing thought. "I'm sorry you wasted your time coming here just for that. I thanked Megan for the invite yesterday but told her it would be best if I didn't attend any of your family functions."

"Why? Are you saying the only reason you got to know my family was because of me?"

"No, if you'll recall, I knew Megan and your sisters long before I met you. However, considering our history, I thought distance was best."

Zane stared at her. "I don't understand why you would think that now when you had no problem attending Megan's wedding and bringing 'Roving Eyes' with you."

Channing's frown deepened. "First of all, Megan is

a good friend of mine, and I saw nothing wrong with being there to share in her happiness. And, for the second time, my fiancé's name is Mack."

Zane leaned back against a table and kept his gaze fixed on hers. "Didn't it bother you that *Mack* was checking out other women with you right by his side? And don't say you weren't aware of it, because you're too astute not to have been."

She shrugged. "All men check out other women. Big deal. Are you saying you never looked twice at another woman while we were together?"

He sputtered out a harsh laugh. "Hell, yes, that's exactly what I'm saying. I might be an ass when it comes to some things, Channing, but I would never have disrespected you that way. While we were together, I never once looked at another woman. You were everything I needed."

The next words were out of her mouth before she could call them back. "Evidently not, Zane. Had I been everything you needed then I wouldn't be engaged to marry another man."

She saw the anger that flared in his eyes and knew she'd made a direct hit. She might have been everything he needed in the bedroom, but she hadn't been in all the ways that mattered.

"Goodbye, Zane." She walked around him as she headed for the door.

A few days later, Zane stood on the porch of his cousin Dillon's home. It was Friday night chow-down, when all the Westmorelands in Denver got together. The women cooked, and the men came hungry. Although they all lived in what was considered Westmoreland Country, they didn't get to see each other every day.

The chow-down was a way to bring everyone up to date on what was happening with each family member.

Seldom was anyone outside of family invited, but Zane hadn't thought twice about making Channing a regular during the nine months they'd dated. His family liked her, and she'd gotten along with everyone—especially the womenfolk. After a while, they'd begun to consider her one of them. That was when his troubles began.

Channing had gotten ideas about them sharing a future. Somewhere along the way, she'd figured he had fallen in love and was rethinking his position on marriage. She'd found out the hard way that Zane Westmoreland didn't change easily.

"You've been pretty quiet all evening."

Zane glanced over his shoulder as his brother Ramsey stepped outside to join him. After dinner, the women retired to the family room to watch a chick flick, and, like usual after such a delicious meal, the men gathered in the game room for drinks and poker. But Zane hadn't been in the mood. He had come out to get a breath of fresh air.

"I've had a rough week with the horses," he said, knowing that was only part of the reason for his mood. "Sugar Plum had to be transported to Casey, Visa Girl got loose and ran wild for a few hours, and Born Free had a difficult delivery."

Ramsey chuckled as he came to stand beside Zane. "That's all?"

"Isn't that enough?"

Ramsey didn't say anything for a minute and then, "Not for Zane Westmoreland, who thrives on challenges and difficulties. Why don't you tell me the real reason for your surly mood?"

Zane didn't say anything for a long moment. "Channing's back in town."

"So I heard."

Zane flashed an accusing gaze at his brother. "And you didn't tell me, either?"

"I only heard she was back this morning. Chloe mentioned it over breakfast. I understand she was invited to dinner tonight but declined."

"Nobody told me she was back. I should have been prepared," Zane muttered.

Ramsey lifted a brow. "Prepared? Why? You saw her last month at Megan's wedding."

"That was then. This is now."

"What makes 'now' different, Zane?" Ramsey asked. "I assumed you'd pretty much made up your mind two years ago when you let her go. You said you didn't want Channing in your life."

"That's not true," Zane snapped.

Ramsey lifted a brow, not anticipating such a strong response. "Then what is true?"

Zane paused and then said, "She wanted more than I could give."

Ramsey frowned. "Did she want more than you could give, or was it that you refused to give her more?"

Zane heaved out a deep, frustrated breath. "Channing knew the score, Ram. Love is not in my vocabulary. She knew that and accepted my terms. Then, months later, she tried changing the game, but there was no way I was going along with it."

"So, in other words, you wanted her as your lover but had no intention of ever allowing her to be more than that. You would have been satisfied to keep a casual arrangement for another two, three, possibly four years? Forever? Damn it, Zane, how would you feel if

Rico would have wanted that kind of relationship with Megan, or Callum with Gemma? Yet you had no problem wanting one with Channing."

"I don't love her like Rico loves Megan and Callum loves Gemma," Zane said, narrowing his eyes. "And I wasn't going to lie to her and say I did."

Ramsey shook his head. "Then I don't blame Channing for leaving. You let her know she was nothing more than another notch on your bedpost."

"She accepted my terms like all my other lovers," Zane snapped. "She knew the score. We couldn't have the kind of future she wanted because I didn't love her."

"If you really didn't have feelings for her, you wouldn't have moped around for months after she left, and you wouldn't be all tied up in knots about her being in Denver now," Ramsey muttered. He shook his head and added, "Well, it doesn't matter now since she's engaged."

"He doesn't deserve her," Zane said in a voice sparked with anger.

"At least the man is willing to give her something you wouldn't—to make her a permanent part of his life."

"Damn it, Ramsey. You saw how he was looking at other women at Megan's wedding. He's going to end up hurting her."

"And you didn't?" When Zane didn't respond, Ramsey didn't say anything else for a minute and then said, "I wasn't going to mention this to you because it's really none of my business, but..."

Zane raised a brow. "What's none of your business?"

"I overheard a conversation between Megan and Chloe yesterday."

"About what?"

"Channing's fiancé. Tara called from Atlanta and

told Megan she saw the man last week and remembered him from the wedding as Channing's fiancé. He was out on the town with women in intimate settings on two separate occasions." Tara was married to their cousin Thorn and they lived in Atlanta.

Zane swore through gritted teeth. In a way, he wasn't surprised about what Tara had seen. But what did surprise him was the fact that Channing refused to accept that her fiancé was a womanizer.

"Like I said, he doesn't deserve her," Zane said. "I might not have loved her, but I would never have betrayed her the way he's doing."

Ramsey nodded. "I'm going back inside. Are you coming?"

Zane shook his head. "No, I'm calling it a night. Think I might even sleep in late tomorrow. I haven't done that on a Saturday in a long time."

"All right. But you'll be joining us for Sunday's dinner, right? Susan's going to be upset if she doesn't see her uncle Zane there," Ramsey said, smiling.

Zane thought about his niece, who would be turning four soon. The niece he adored. "I won't disappoint her. I'll be there," he said, moving down the steps. "Tell the others good-night for me."

"Hey, babe, are you missing me? All you have to do is say the word and I'll fly out there and give you all the attention you deserve."

Channing rolled her eyes, bristling at Mack Hammond's words. "Cut it out, Mack. Need I remind you what happened last month at Megan's wedding? You couldn't keep your eyes off the women. Now you have everyone thinking I'm engaged to a womanizing jerk."

"Hey, you didn't warn me there would be so many

beautiful women there. It was quite obvious your ex-boyfriend didn't like the fact that you returned to town an engaged woman."

Mack was right. Zane hadn't been happy about it. If their conversation at the hospital was anything to go on, he still wasn't. "But did you have to check them out so obviously? You don't believe in the word *subtle,* do you?" she asked, trying not to smile.

She had met Mack within weeks of arriving in Atlanta two years ago. They had dated a few times, but when he saw she would not put up with his playboy foolishness, they had become good friends instead. A few months ago, when he'd been invited to a cousin's wedding, he'd asked her to pretend to be his fiancée to keep his matchmaking parents and grandparents off his back. Then, when Channing had received the invitation to Megan's wedding, Mack had returned the favor. The last thing she'd wanted was to return to Denver alone and looking pathetic.

The only person who knew the truth about her fake engagement was Megan, who had found the entire ploy hilarious. She'd said there was no reason for Channing to end the charade since it really wasn't any of Zane's business.

"So, have you seen Zane Westmoreland yet?" Mack asked.

Catching her lower lip between her teeth, Channing eased down onto the sofa and curled up in a comfortable position. "Yes, he stopped by the lecture hall a few days ago. He figured I would be dropping by his family's place for dinner while I was in town, and he said we needed to clear the air so things wouldn't be uncomfortable."

"Uncomfortable for whom? You or him?"

"Both, I imagine. But I told him he didn't have to worry about that. I have no intention of attending any of his family's gatherings."

"Was he relieved to hear it?"

Channing shrugged. "Not sure, but it really doesn't matter. He's moved on and so have I. I'm over Zane."

"Are you?"

Channing frowned. "Yes. Why would you doubt it?"

"I'll give you my answer the next time I see you. Have you decided when that will be?"

"Not yet. Class enrollment here is high. I've been here almost three weeks already and Dr. Rowe wants me to consider doing another three-week class. I haven't decided on anything yet."

"Well, I know whatever decision you make will be the right one," he said. "Take care and be good."

"Same back at you, Mack."

Channing clicked off the phone and tried to force the conversation with Zane out of her mind. Nothing about him had changed. He still wanted to be footloose and fancy-free, and she still wanted the whole shebang— love, marriage and family.

She had lied just now to Mack when she claimed that she was over Zane. She'd honestly believed she was, but all it had taken was seeing him again to be proved wrong. Just being in the same room with him had stirred memories and emotions she knew were better kept undisturbed.

The most she could hope for was that her path and Zane's wouldn't cross again.

Megan caught hold of Chloe Westmoreland's arm and pulled her into the kitchen. "Do you think Ramsey took the bait yesterday?"

A smile touched Chloe's lips. "I'm sure he did. You and I were talking loud enough. And tonight was the perfect time for him to tell Zane just what he overheard. In fact, Ramsey just came back inside from being out on the porch with Zane, and when I asked where Zane had gone off to, Ramsey said Zane went home, calling it an early night because he'd had a bad week."

"I bet," Megan said, chuckling. "Especially since he found out Channing is back in town."

"I hope you're right about how Zane feels about her," Chloe said in a low voice. "What about Channing? Will she be upset when she finds out we stuck our noses into her affairs?"

"In the end, both Zane and Channing will get what they truly want, which is each other. Zane moped around like a sick puppy when Channing left for Atlanta, but he was too darn stubborn to recognize his true feelings. If he loves Channing like I believe he does, then the one thing he won't stand for is someone hurting her. Zane is very protective of those he cares about. He's going to come up with a plan to save her from Mack."

"What do you think he'll do?" Chloe asked.

Now that was a good question, Megan thought. Zane was the brother who was usually too logical for his own good. The same one who made it his business to know everything there was to know about women. The family should have known they would be in trouble when Zane decided to major in psychology in college. "I'm not sure. We'll just have to wait and see."

Three

The next morning, Zane sat on the edge of the bed, holding the locked box. After looking at it for a long moment, he slid it back underneath. He had been tempted to go through its contents once again.

He rubbed his hand over his face, feeling tired, although he had gotten into bed way before midnight. But he hadn't gotten much sleep, and upon awakening this morning, he had lain there, gazing up at the ceiling and thinking about Channing.

The thought of any man betraying her twisted his gut with anger. No woman deserved that, which was why he was always up front with any woman he was involved with. Channing hadn't been an exception. He had set the same ground rules with her as he had with other women, and, like he'd told Ramsey, she had accepted his terms.

He truly hadn't meant for their involvement to last

as long as it had, and more than once he'd considered breaking it off sooner instead of later. But each time he felt pressed to do so—whenever he was getting too comfortable and relaxed—he would change his mind.

He enjoyed Channing both in and out of the bedroom. She had been fun to be with. Unlike others he'd dated, she wasn't a hard woman to please, which somehow made him want to please her more. She'd gotten next to him in a way no other female had: the way a smile could tease across her lips, her special scent that could drive him wild with lust or just plain spending time with her. She'd had a way of making him smile when he didn't want to be amused, a way of bringing him out. She was someone he could talk to for hours. One thing he missed more than anything else was their late-night phone conversations.

On those nights when she'd stayed late at the hospital, he would come home, shower and wait on her call. When it came, they would chat well into the night. She would tell him how her day went, and he would tell her about his. Then they would move into a number of other topics. It had been a special connection, one he'd hated losing.

And then there were those hot and sexy text messages she would send him during the day. They had come up with their own code, and she would tell him what to expect next time he saw her. And she would deliver.

Now she was engaged to marry someone else.

He should wish her well. She was just one woman, and he had dated others since her. But he would be the first to admit that his time with those other women just hadn't been the same. He had been enchanted by Channing from the beginning. She was a softhearted and passionate woman who brightened up any room. She was in a class by herself, and it bothered the hell out of him that she planned to marry a man who thought nothing of betraying her.

He stood and headed toward the kitchen. "Leave it alone, Zane. It's not your problem," he muttered to himself. He'd tried convincing himself of that very thing on his drive home from the family dinner last night. But as much as he told himself he wanted to wash his hands of Channing because she didn't matter, he knew she did.

Seeing her again a few days ago had reignited feelings he had tried to deny. He had missed her, and damn it all, he still wanted her. He'd never invaded another man's territory when it came to a woman, but this was different. Like he'd told Ramsey, the bastard didn't deserve her.

If he knew where she was staying, he would pay her a visit and try to talk some sense into her. But he didn't know, and he would not ask Megan. That meant he had to show up at the hospital again—with a plan.

Channing stopped when she saw Zane standing in the hospital parking lot, leaning on a light pole with his legs crossed at the ankles and his Stetson positioned low on his head. What was he doing here? Was he waiting for her? Why?

There had been a time when the sight of him would have had her heart jumping in her chest, and she was feeling annoyed with the fact that nothing had changed as far as that was concerned. She had been gone for almost two years, and at Megan's wedding, he'd gone out of his way to ignore her. Now she was back in town, and in only a week's time he had sought her out twice.

And each time he'd done so, she was reminded just how deeply she had fallen in love with Zane.

She was finding it harder and harder to put aside her emotions when dealing with him. No one had ever warned her that falling in love would be so painstakingly complicated.

"Zane."

He straightened to his full six-foot-three-inch height. "Channing. I've been waiting for you."

She stared up at him. "Obviously."

"We need to talk." He pushed his hat back from his face, fully uncovering his eyes.

She wished he hadn't done that. Now she was staring into the eyes that had haunted her on so many nights. The eyes that would darken whenever they made love. The eyes with the intensity to turn her on with one heated glanced.

Channing drew in a deep breath when she felt a tingling sensation stir in her stomach. "We have nothing to talk about, Zane."

His brows creased in a thoughtful expression as he stared down at her. She couldn't help but wonder what he was thinking. It had been rumored that when it came to women that Zane was all knowing, and she'd pretty much discovered that to be true. He could tell each and every time she'd wanted him to make love to her, saying he could read her like a book. She wondered if he was trying to read her now. Lord, she hoped not. The last thing she needed was for him to know that just standing here with him made her nipples harden against her bra and threaded a tingling sensation through her bloodstream.

"I think we do," he said in a deep, husky tone that set her nerves on edge.

Bitterness tightened her lips. "Why?"

"I prefer to talk over a meal."

Her gaze lifted. "A meal?"

He cocked his head to the side. "Yes, a meal. You haven't had dinner yet and neither have I. There's no reason why we can't share one together. If nothing else, I'd like to think we're still friends."

Friends? Boy was he wrong. "Look, Zane, I don't know what this is all about, but the last thing you and I need to do is rekindle any friendship."

He crossed his arms over his chest. "Why? Are you worried what good old Mack will say if he finds out you had dinner with me? Seems to me that he probably trusts you a lot more than you should trust him."

She narrowed her gaze at him. "I'm not going to bother asking what you mean by that."

"No, you won't, but maybe you should."

Channing stared down at her shoes. She desperately needed to break eye contact with him. Zane was starting to wear on her last nerve. Thinking she had herself together, she returned her gaze to his. "Why are you so concerned about my relationship with Mack, Zane? You had your chance."

Zane sighed and dropped his hands to his sides. "Look, will it kill you to have dinner with me?"

"To talk?"

"Yes, to talk."

Channing studied her shoes again. What harm could come of her having dinner with him? Although he might not like Mack, the one thing Zane would not do was trespass on another man's territory. He assumed she was an engaged woman, so that would keep him in line. Besides, she was curious about what he wanted to discuss.

"Fine, we'll talk," she said, looking back up at him.

He still carried a chip on his shoulder because of how she'd left. Maybe it was time they hashed things out once and for all.

"We can go in my car, and I'll bring you back here," Zane said.

There was no way she would say yes to being alone with him in a car for any length of time. "No thanks, I can drive my own car and follow you."

He looked as if he wanted to argue, but she figured her expression made him think twice. "Fine, we're going to McKays," he said.

She went still. McKays was a well-known restaurant in town, and she had once considered it their place since they dined there often.

She lifted her chin. "I'll follow."

The moment they walked into McKays, Zane knew he should have suggested another place. Denver wasn't a small city by any stretch of the word, but the people who frequented McKays were regulars, and the Westmorelands were well-known in these parts.

The majority of these people had known Zane, his siblings and his cousins all their lives. And Zane figured most remembered him and Channing coming here together quite a few times. That was probably the reason the two of them drew so much attention as the waitress led them to a table in the middle of the restaurant.

"We need something a little more private, Tasha," he told their waitress when he saw they would be sitting across from a woman who was straining her neck to stare at them.

"No problem," Tasha said, smiling as she led them in another direction. "I have the perfect table for you two."

Channing glanced over at him and said nothing, althougth he knew what she was probably thinking. Tasha had been their regular waitress two years ago. No doubt Tasha saw some great significance with them eating together again after so long. And the engagement ring on Channing's finger was probably giving Tasha further misconceptions.

He smiled his approval when Tasha led them into a private room in the back. Although it was larger than what they needed, it was perfect. He would be able to hold a conversation with Channing without fear of being overheard. However, he could tell from the look on Channing's face that she didn't particularly like the intimate setting.

"I'm not going to bite, you know," he said, pulling out the chair for her after Tasha had left them alone.

Sitting down, she glanced over her shoulder at him, and he saw a fragment of a smile touch her lips. "Promise?"

Instead of moving away, he leaned down and whispered close to her ear, "Um, I don't know now. You do look good enough to eat."

A shiver passed through Channing when Zane moved away to take his seat. Erotic images flooded her brain, and she achingly remembered a time or two when he'd done exactly that—practically made a meal out of her.

She placed her napkin in her lap and noticed him staring at her. It didn't help matters that he had the most arresting eyes, and at that moment, they were filled with intensity. Zane was a powerfully sensuous man, and there was no doubt in her mind that he knew it. Men didn't draw women to them in droves the way he did and not know about their own magnetism.

Tasha returned and placed water, a bottle of their usual choice in wine and menus in front of them, said something about coming back later to take their order and then left them alone again. Zane continued to stare as he opened the wine bottle and poured them a glass, and—unable to do anything else—Channing stared back at him. She could feel the heat of his gaze touching every part of her, even parts he couldn't see.

Raw emotions she'd forced away for two years slowly returned. She felt her skin grow warm under the goose bumps forming on her arms. Then there was the smell of his cologne. She recognized the fragrance. It was one she had purchased for him as a Christmas gift. The masculine scent drove sensuous shivers up her spine.

What was he trying to do to her? What was he trying to make her feel? She was assailed with sensations she only felt while around him: that sinfully seductive consciousness washing passion through her, intense degrees of longing pulsating through her body.

Drawing in a deep breath, she broke eye contact with him and picked up her menu. Whatever it took, she must not forget that he was Zane, the man she had fallen in love with, the same man who had told her that he enjoyed sleeping with her but didn't love her. He could never love her, and she wanted a man who could.

When she glanced back up at him, he was still staring, which prompted her to ignore the racing of her pulse long enough to ask, "Have you forgotten that I'm engaged to someone?"

She watched as he took a slow swallow of his wine and then licked his lips before answering her.

"No, I haven't forgotten. Although I would like to," he said in a deep, husky voice. "I was just sitting here remembering all the good times we had together."

A shudder worked its way through her body as she remembered those good times, as well. Within a week of being introduced, they had shared a bed. That was unusual for her because she wasn't the type to become involved in meaningless relationships. But she'd been like most women who'd found him addictive: Zane's masculine charm had lured her in, conjuring up illusions that he was falling in love with her as much as she was with him. At the end, she'd found out the hard way just how wrong she'd been. Two years later and she could still feel the aftershocks of a broken heart.

"They were good times, weren't they?" he asked softly, breaking into her thoughts.

She gazed into dark, mesmerizing eyes. Whether she wanted to admit it or not, those had been good times. Candlelit dinners. Sex so hot it burned the sheets. And a closeness she'd never felt with any other man. "Yes, Zane, they were good, but those times are over and done with."

There, he needed to know she'd moved on. But had she really? She wanted to think she had, even though she hadn't been involved in another affair—serious or otherwise—since him. But that was beside the point. The main point was that Zane had never loved her and never would.

She was saved from any further conversation between them when Tasha returned to take their dinner order.

Zane took his time eating; he was in no hurry to broach the subject he had brought Channing here to discuss. At the moment, he was satisfied just indulging in small talk. He'd told her how the family was gearing up for his cousin Riley's wedding in September and how the horse breeding and training business was going. He talked about Bailey and how annoying his kid sister could still be at times, and he brought her up to date on Bane and how proud they were that his cousin was officially a navy SEAL.

Every so often he couldn't help but stare at her. She was so incredibly beautiful. How could any man not appreciate the woman she was? Now, two years too late, he himself could admit he had not appreciated her. He had enjoyed her, admired her and lusted after her. But he hadn't appreciated her. He would have been happy for their relationship to remain the same—without considering her wants and needs. Without considering what she deserved.

She deserved a man who appreciated her. He hadn't done so, and it looked as though her fiancé wasn't, either.

"I understand from Megan there might be some more Westmorelands out there somewhere," Channing said, breaking into his thoughts.

He looked at her, and another dose of desire tightened his groin. Her hair was pulled back and pinned on top of her head in a knot. A few tendrils had escaped confinement and brushed against her cheek. She was wearing a skirt and blouse; the color of both brought out the hazel of her eyes. There had always been a powerful attraction between them. He would have thought it had eroded by now. It hadn't.

She had to be aware of how charged the air was. She was trying to downplay it, but he felt that tug each and every time their gazes met. To know the attraction was still strong engulfed him in one hell of a delicious feeling. She might be engaged to marry another man, but there was no doubt in his mind she was still drawn to him. How was he supposed to concentrate on his meal with that kind of knowledge nudging up his testosterone?

"Yes," he said, taking a sip of wine. "During Megan and Rico's trip to Texas, they found evidence of a child my great-grandfather Raphel never knew he had. That child was given up to a woman right before the mother died in a train wreck. There was little for Rico to go on since few records were kept during that time. We're talking about more than seventy years ago. But Rico was able to get a listing of every passenger on the train—those who survived and those who didn't. He's still weeding through all of that information now. I'm told it was an extensive passenger list."

Channing nodded. "All of you must be pleased with how the investigation is going, though."

"Yes, we are. I'm confident Rico will eventually find our relatives. He's good at what he does, but it will take time. And there's still another woman who was assumed to be Raphel's fourth wife, Isabelle Connors. Rico is investigating any clues associated with her, as well."

As they continued their meal, he brought her up to date on all the babies who had been born to his cousins, the Atlanta Westmorelands. She had met most of them when they'd come to town for his sister Gemma's wedding.

"How's your folks?" he asked her.

He'd never met her parents or any of her family members since the Hastings lived in New Hampshire, but she would speak of them often and fondly. "They're fine. My brother's employer moved him to San Diego last year, and he loves it there."

Channing finished her meal and paused before asking, "So what did you want to talk to me about?"

She felt the intensity of his gaze once again.

"It's about the mistake you're making."

She lifted a brow. "What mistake?"

Zane took another sip of his wine. For some reason, she was willing to accept Mack Hammond and all his flaws, but Zane refused to let her be that generous. He placed his glass down on the table. "Marrying a man you don't love," he said calmly.

Fire flashed in her eyes. "And what makes you think I don't love Mack?"

A smile touched his lips as he leaned in closer. "Because I know you, Channing. If you loved him, you would not be sitting over there getting as aroused as I am."

Four

Channing gaped. "Aroused?"

"Yes."

She frowned. "I'm not aroused." The sudden rush of heat between her legs made a liar out of her, but she would never admit it.

"Yes, you are," Zane said with certainty. "Do you want me to prove it?"

"No, because you can't."

"You think not?" he asked, sliding his chair back and standing up.

Channing recognized that look in his eyes and drew in a sharp breath. "What is wrong with you, Zane?" She held up her ringed finger, slowly waving it for him to see. "Doesn't this mean anything to you?"

"Not a damn thing."

He reached behind him to lock the door before moving around the table. She quickly stood and backed up.

"I don't know what's gotten into you, but I refuse to put up with this foolishness. I'm leaving."

When she moved toward the door, he grabbed her hand. The moment he touched her, she froze, then a flood of desire rampaged through her bloodstream, making mush of her already stretched-to-the-limit senses.

"You think you're not aroused, Channing," he drawled, leaning in close. His tongue teased her lips, and she knew she had to stop things from going any further.

"I'm an engaged woman," she tried saying in outrage.

"You're an engaged woman who wants me," he countered. "Admit it."

"I won't admit a thing."

He shrugged. "Then feel," he whispered as his fingers traced up her arm.

Channing fought back a lustful moan as pleasure swept across the skin he touched. "I don't want to feel."

"Your body is saying otherwise. Why is that, Channing?"

She shook her head, fighting off the way his eyes were mesmerizing her. "You're wrong."

"No, sweetheart, I'm right, and I intend to show you just how right I am." He pulled her close, leaned in and swooped down on her mouth.

Push him away, damn it, Channing's mind screamed.

But at the first taste of his tongue her mind changed course and began chanting, *Devour him like he's devouring you, and don't let go.*

So she didn't.

Moments later, she wasn't exactly sure whose tongue was dominating or at what point they had begun pulling off each other's clothes. What was happening here? Invading another man's territory was not Zane's style.

Before she could question his actions any further, air hit her skin, and she realized she was halfway naked and so was he. She pulled her mouth from his. "Zane, you're not thinking straight. We need to—"

Whatever she was about to say vanished from her lips when he dropped to his knees and latched his hot mouth on her. Before Zane, oral sex had been something she read about in romance novels, but Zane had brought it to life for her. The man had a skillful mouth.

She clasped her hands on his shoulders, intending to shove him back, but at the feel of his hungry tongue, she let out a lusty moan. She instinctively arched her back and pushed herself into his mouth.

He knew all the erogenous spots to claim, conquer and satisfy.

"Zane!"

As sensations zapped her, he stroked his tongue across her, slanting his mouth at different angles. Each stroke had her moaning deep in her throat and whispering his name through her lips. And then it happened— an avalanche of the kind of pleasure she found only with him ripped through her. Instead of letting her go, he grabbed tightly to her thighs and held on as a cavalcade of spasms overtook her.

The next thing she knew, he was lifting her and placing her on one of the vacant tables and spreading her out. When she watched him rip open a condom packet with his teeth, she knew what he intended to do. Instead of stopping him, she reached down and grabbed his throbbing erection. It was just as she remembered— large, thick and nesting in a thatch of dark, curly hair. An urgency she hadn't felt in two years came over her, and she whispered in a heated breath, "I need you inside me. Now!"

He quickly slid on the condom and then, while staring into her eyes, he thrust inside of her, quickly setting a rhythm with deep, powerful strokes. He went deep, then deeper and took her to the hilt.

She moaned as her body became carnally reacquainted with his. Zane was a master at giving pleasure, and he was bequeathing a generous dose on her. She felt his swollen shaft each time he moved. She felt it all: how her feminine muscles clamped tightly on every inch of him, trying to drain him of everything he had.

Then, suddenly, an explosion of pleasure hit her. She would have let out a wail if he hadn't firmly locked his mouth on hers. Her response triggered him, and he pounded into her harder and deeper as her powerful orgasm ripped into her, nearly jerking her body off the table.

How could something so wrong feel so right? She pushed the question from her mind as his climax began and she was given yet another orgasm.

He snatched his mouth from hers and threw his head back, growling hoarsely, a sound she would admit she'd missed. She curved her arms around his neck to bring his mouth back down to hers. And then she kissed him—the way a woman was supposed to kiss a man who meant the world to her.

When she released him, he stared down at her, smiled and whispered, "Damn, I missed this. I missed you."

She didn't say anything but instead closed her eyes. Her common sense came reeling back with a vengeance as he eased himself out of her and then gently helped her off the table. They'd had spontaneous sex before but never in a public place. They were in a restaurant in downtown Denver, for heaven's sake! She didn't want to think about how many times Tasha might have tried to open the locked door. Had anyone heard them?

"Do you need help getting back into your clothes?"

She jerked her gaze over to where Zane stood. He had his clothes back on like he had never taken them off. "No, I can handle it," she said softly, picking up her panties from the floor.

When she began sliding the undergarment up her legs, his next words stopped her. "How soon will you be breaking your engagement to Hammond?"

There was something about the way he'd asked, something about the tone of his voice that made her gut twist in a knot. He spoke as if her engagement had been a problem he'd solved. Had he? Dread consumed her.

"What makes you think I'm ending my engagement?" she asked, deciding to play her hunch and hope like hell that she was wrong. Surely he hadn't seduced her just to force her to break her engagement?

"Of course you're going to break it. You're not the type of woman who would be engaged to one man and mess around with another."

No, she wasn't. "And you're not the type of man to mess around with a woman who's not yours. A woman who belongs to another man. I guess we've both acted out of character today."

She watched his face take on a formidable look when he said, "I didn't act out of character, sweetheart. I was merely proving a point."

She had finished dressing now, and his words gave her pause. "Just what point were you trying to prove?"

He slowly crossed the room and pinned her against the table by bracing his arms on either side of her. He leaned in to get eye level with her. "The point I *proved* is that you're mine. There's no other man for you but me, and I don't intend to give you up."

Channing forced her heart to *not* leap with joy. Did that mean he loved her after all? He had yet to say the words. She decided to ask him straight-out. "Does that mean you realized you love me?"

He actually seemed shocked at her assumption. He straightened. "No. It means I care for you, and I don't want to see you get hurt. Hammond would have hurt you."

Pain ripped through Channing, and her heart twisted. Did he not realize *he* was hurting her? "Let me get this straight," she said, fighting anger. "You don't love me but you brought me here to seduce me just to prove a point?"

Zane frowned. "I brought you here to talk some sense into you, but I ended up seducing some sense into you instead. Doing so brought back some damn pleasant memories, don't you think?"

She swallowed, suddenly feeling like the biggest fool on the planet. "So you only had sex with me because you figured I would have no choice but to break off my engagement?" she asked softly.

He shook his head. "No, I made love to you because I wanted you, and it was obvious you wanted me, as well. That made me realize you couldn't possibly love Hammond if you desired me. I was right. Your body wants me, so the way I see it, you belong to me."

She closed her eyes as blood rushed to her head. "Now that I belong to you, Zane, what do you plan to do with me? You just admitted once again that you don't love me, which means you don't intend to marry me. So what are you going to do with me, Zane?"

When he didn't say anything, when he just stood

there staring at her with a deep scowl on his face, her anger exploded. "You selfish jerk! You don't want to give me all the things I want—love, marriage and a family—yet you don't want any other man to give me those things, either!"

"Damn it, Channing! Hammond is fooling around on you. I didn't want him to hurt you. You don't need to marry a man like that."

"You're the only who has ever hurt me, Zane," she said as pain etched itself all through her body. "You don't love me, but you don't want any other man to love me."

Zane gritted his teeth. "Didn't you hear what I said? Hammond is being unfaithful to you."

"No, he isn't," she said sharply. "I was never engaged to Mack. I only pretended to be. Mack is a good friend and nothing more. But you didn't know that. For all you knew, he could have been my happiness, but you still went so far as to try to destroy that."

Shock shone on Zane's face. "What do you mean you were never engaged to him?"

Instead of answering, Channing moved toward the door. Fighting back tears, she unlocked it, snatched it open and quickly walked out.

Five

Later that night, Zane flung his front door open to find an angry Megan on his doorstep. "It's too late for visitors, Megan, and I'm not in the mood," he said in a low growl.

His sister pushed her way past him, strode to the middle of his living room and angrily whirled to face him. "If you weren't my brother, and if I had a gun, I would shoot you in the balls right here and now."

He felt the pain of her words and his balls ached in response. "Go ahead and say what you have to say so I can get some sleep."

"Sleep! How can you sleep after what you did to Channing?"

He crossed his arms over his chest. "She had no reason to call you. She lied about her engagement. She was never going to marry that guy with the roving eyes, but you knew that all along, didn't you? You not only invited her to the wedding when I pleaded with you not to but you let her make a fool of me."

Megan rounded on him, and he had the good sense to back up. An angry, out-of-control Gemma or Bailey he could deal with but an angry Megan he could not. Everyone knew about her penchant for self-control. On those rare times when she lost it, she was a force to reckon with.

"First of all, Channing didn't call me. Louise Mitchell did," Megan snapped.

"Louise Mitchell?"

"Yes, as well as Emma Falk and Mavis Upshaw. They were all dining at McKays when Channing practically ran out of the private room in tears. I immediately went to see Channing when I got off work tonight. Thanks to you, she was completely devastated. She told me everything, Zane. *Everything*. And if you weren't my brother, I would shoot you."

"Not if I shot him first."

Zane looked toward his front door where an angry Bailey had let herself in. The hellion! That was all he needed. "You are supposed to knock, Bailey."

"Kiss it, Zane." She glanced over at Megan. "I heard. Wanda Grunthall's parents were dining at McKays."

Zane rolled his eyes. Was there anyone who hadn't been dining at McKays tonight? "If the two of you want to discuss my business among yourselves then go ahead. I'm going to bed."

"The hell you will," Bailey said, moving toward him. "You're going to sit and listen to what we have to say. And don't be surprised if Gemma calls you from Australia. Wanda Grunthall is a good friend of hers, as well."

Seeing that he would never get to bed until he heard

what his sisters had to say, he dropped down on the sofa. "Okay, I'm giving you both five minutes. Say what you have to say and leave."

Megan went first. "Have you even taken the time to consider why someone like Channing would fake an engagement?"

"I don't have to wonder why. She did it to piss me off."

"It's not all about you!" Bailey shouted.

Zane flinched. He was sick and tired of being yelled at. "If you use that tone of voice again in my presence, Bailey, I'm going to snatch up your little butt, take you to the bathroom and wash your mouth out with soap like I used to do."

Bailey glared at him. "Go to—"

"Bailey!" Megan interrupted. "Please let me finish. Then you can go for blood if you want."

Bailey nodded. "Sorry. Please continue, Megan."

Megan smiled at her sister. "Thanks." She then narrowed her gaze at Zane. "No, Zane, that's not the reason. Channing did it to keep her dignity and pride in check when she came to town for my wedding. Two years ago, when you were dating, people talked, made bets, laughed at her behind her back and figured you would eventually kick her to the curb like you did all the others."

Zane's jaw tightened. His eyes sparked fire. "Who told you that?"

"Doesn't matter. Everyone around these parts knows your reputation when it comes to women. But Channing hung in there because she thought she meant more to you than that. Most people knew better. They knew she really didn't mean a damn thing to you, that eventually you would drop her and move on."

Megan paused. "She was your steady girlfriend for nine months, Zane. Although I'm certain you gave her the same warning that you gave all your other women, at some point she began thinking she might be different. We all did. You treated her differently from the rest."

Zane didn't say anything for a long minute and then said quietly, "She was different."

"Then why would you hurt her, Zane? All you wanted to do was prove a point? What if Rico had done something like that to me?"

Before he could answer, Bailey spoke up and asked, "What did Zane do to Channing? All Wanda said was that they had a little spat. Is there more?"

Both Zane and Megan said simultaneously, "No."

Bailey narrowed her eyes. "You two are lying."

Instead of responding to Bailey's accusations, Megan returned her attention to Zane. "She told me the truth about the fake engagement, and I feel partly to blame for what happened because I deliberately let Ramsey eavesdrop on a conversation I had with Chloe. I figured he would tell you what Mack Hammond was doing and that you would get upset about it and come up with a plan to save Channing. Lord knows, I didn't think you'd go as far as you did."

"Damn, what did he do?" Bailey asked again.

A collective "nothing" was the response from Megan and Zane.

Then Zane said to Megan, "It wasn't planned. It just happened."

"Ahh," Bailey said, figuring out what nobody was telling her. An angry frown settled on her face. "If you weren't my brother, I would castrate you."

Zane rolled his eyes, although he believed Bailey was more likely to carry out her threat than Megan was.

"I never meant to hurt her," he said, when he began to realize just what had happened. He had tried to stop Hammond from hurting Channing, and he was the one guilty of causing her pain.

"I need to go see her and apologize," he said, standing.

"Too late," Megan said softly. "By the time I'd gotten over to her place, she had already canceled the rest of her symposium and packed her things. I sat and talked to her until it was time for her to leave for the airport."

Zane felt a gut-wrenching sensation in the pit of his stomach. "She's left town?"

"Do you blame her, Zane?" Megan asked.

He drew in a deep breath. No, he didn't blame her. "Doesn't matter. I'm leaving for Atlanta tomorrow."

Megan placed her hands on her hips. "To do what? Tell her you're sorry for what you did but that you still don't love her? Just let her go, Zane. You've done enough damage. Besides, she's not going to Atlanta."

He lifted a brow. "Where did she go, Megan?" he asked in a near growl.

"Don't tell him," Bailey piped in to say. "He will only hurt her again. Channing wants to be loved, and Zane isn't capable of loving any woman."

Zane ignored Bailey's words and continued to hold Megan's gaze. "Did she go to her parents' in New Hampshire?" he asked.

"Don't tell him, Megan!"

Megan drew in a deep breath. "No, she didn't go there, either."

Zane felt an intense need to ferret out her location. All of Channing's family lived in New Hampshire. He then remembered that she'd told him her brother had moved to San Diego. "Did she go to California?"

"No."

"Then where the hell did she go?"

Megan lifted her chin. "If you find out Channing's whereabouts, it won't be with my help. Bailey's right. You're not capable of loving anyone but yourself, so just leave her alone."

She turned and headed for the door. After giving him one hard glare, Bailey followed her sister.

Early the next morning, after a sleepless night—and when he was certain Megan had left for work—Zane got in his truck and headed over to Megan's Meadows to see Rico. His brother-in-law opened the door with a sympathetic look on his face. "I heard my wife tore into you pretty damn good last night."

Zane grunted as he strolled toward the kitchen, following the aroma of coffee. He went still when he saw his brother Derringer and his cousins Jason, Riley, Canyon and Stern sitting at the kitchen table. "Somebody gave you guys a day off of work or something?" he asked Riley, Canyon and Stern. The three worked for the family-owned business, Blue Ridge Land Management.

Riley chuckled. "It's still early yet. Besides, we heard both Megan and Bailey chewed you out, and we wanted to be here when you came and asked Rico for a bandage."

Zane set his chin in a frown. "Funny." After helping himself to a cup of coffee, he slid into one of the empty chairs at the table.

"That's not why they're here, Zane," Rico said, grinning, leaning against the counter with his own cup of coffee. "In fact, Ramsey and Dillon are on their way over, as well. I called you earlier this morning to tell you about this impromptu meeting, but you didn't answer the phone."

Zane shrugged. "I thought it was Megan calling, and we don't have anything to say to each other until she tells me where Channing is."

Derringer snorted. "Don't hold your breath for that to happen. Megan's pretty angry with you."

Zane opened his mouth to respond to Derringer's words when there was a knock at the door. "That's probably Ramsey and Dillon," Rico said, moving toward the living room.

Moments later, Ramsey and Dillon Westmoreland walked in and glanced around. Their gazes locked on Zane. Dillon smiled and said, "Glad to see you're still in one piece."

Zane cursed under his breath. Had everybody heard about Megan's and Bailey's visits?

Rico proceeded to get everybody's attention. "I wanted to give you guys an update on something I discovered with Raphel's investigation. I told Megan last night, and now I want to share the information with you."

"What did you find out?" Dillon asked. Since there weren't any more empty seats at the table, he and Ramsey settled their tall frames in stools at the breakfast bar.

"The woman who survived the train wreck and who adopted Raphel's son was Jeannette Outlaw. She named her son Levy—after her husband who was killed in the train accident. She moved to Detroit as a single mother and everyone assumed the child belonged to her deceased husband. She never told anyone anything different."

Rico paused and then continued, "Levy Outlaw married at twenty-five, and he and his wife had one son, Javier. That's where the trail stops. It seems Levy Outlaw, his wife and son moved away from Detroit, but we're not sure of their final destination. My people are working on it."

Rico leaned back against the counter. "The other news I wanted to share is that I found records on a woman by the name of Isabelle Connors who lived in Percy, Nevada. As you all know, Isabelle was documented as Raphel Westmoreland's fourth wife."

"Percy, Nevada?" Dillon asked, lifting a brow. "That's where our great-grandmother Gemma was born and raised. Do you think there's a chance that she and Isabelle knew each other?"

"That's a possibility I'm checking out," Rico said. A smile touched his lips. "Of course Megan is excited about the information I was able to find on Levy Outlaw."

Ramsey grinned as he shook his head. "I bet she was. She's determined to find more cousins to the Westmorelands."

Rico chuckled. "Yes, and don't be surprised if I do."

"I want to know where Channing is, Rico," Zane said after the meeting had ended and everyone had left. "I'm sure Megan told you."

Rico took a sip of his coffee. "Yes, but Megan doesn't think you need to know where Channing is. Your sister believes all you're going to do is hurt her friend again."

Zane didn't say anything. Megan had pretty much made her thoughts damn clear. He had stayed up most of the night, walking the floor. Knowing he had hurt Channing to the point that she had left town had kept him awake. His sisters were right. He had been wrong.

"Zane?"

He glanced over at Rico. "Yes?"

"If you found Channing, what would you do?"

Zane lowered his head and gazed down into his cup of coffee. He had asked himself that same question while walking the floor last night. He would apologize of course, but would that be enough? Lifting his head, he met Rico's gaze. "I'm not sure," he said honestly.

Rico nodded. "Then maybe you should be sure before you go looking for her. When a man goes after a woman, he needs to know why he's doing it. He needs to have a game plan."

Zane didn't say anything, mainly because he'd never needed a game plan when it came to women.

"Do you know at what point I knew I loved your sister, Zane?"

Zane shrugged. He figured there was a reason Rico wanted to tell him this. "No. When?"

"I knew I loved your sister when I realized I couldn't live a single day without her." Rico took a sip of his coffee. "If you ever feel anything close to that kind of emotion, let me know and then I'll tell you where Channing is."

"I'm fine, Megan, really I am. Don't worry. I love it here," Channing said, stepping out onto the porch of her grandparents' oceanside villa in the beautiful Kindle Shores community of Virginia Beach. The house and five others were on a private section of land that developers had been trying to purchase for years. However, like her grandparents, none of the owners were interested in selling.

"It's been a while since I've been here, so maybe Zane did me a favor after all. In addition to reminding me what jerks some men can be, it made me realize I hadn't taken time off from work in a while to rest, relax and regroup," she said, sliding down into the porch swing.

The ocean looked beautiful. As a child, she enjoyed spending her summers here with her grandparents. Adele Hastings hadn't asked any questions when her granddaughter had called saying she needed to come to the house and stay awhile. But Channing had still heard the concern in her grandmother's voice when she'd told Channing where to find the key.

The moment Channing arrived and opened the door a sense of welcome had settled upon her. The memories of the summers she'd spent here were special. It was the time when she and all her cousins would get together to share their grandparents' wisdom and love.

She'd seen how her grandparents had spruced up the place with painted walls, gleaming tile floors and all-new furniture. She liked the look and all the vibrant colors. When it came to decorating, her grandmother still had style.

"Well, if you need anything—and I mean anything at all—call me, Channing," Megan said, interrupting Channing's thoughts. "Again, I'm sorry about everything."

"Don't be. Zane warned me how things would be between us in the very beginning, but I let myself fall in love with him, anyway. As far as the other night at McKays, the desire was mutual. I wanted him, Megan. Your brother proved he's still my weakness. I thought I had gotten over him, but evidently I haven't. He's not a man a woman can forget easily," Channing admitted. "But I will," she added with strong conviction.

"Well, it's going to be a long time before he gets back in my good graces. At some point, he has to come to

terms with the fact that he's going to grow old alone,"
Megan said in a tiff.

A few moments later, after ending her phone call,
Channing stood to stretch and look out at the beach.
The beautiful blue water was inviting, and she decided
she would take a dip later. But for now, she would make
a sandwich and start reading the suspense thriller she
had picked up at the airport.

But once she sat back down, she couldn't help thinking about what had happened over the past couple of
days. Hurt and heartbroken, she had canceled her symposium with apologies and plans to reschedule and had
flown from Denver to here. Upon arriving, she had
gone shopping for enough food for the three weeks she
intended to stay. On the first day, she had called Zane
every god-awful name in the book. Then she'd called
herself a damn fool and indulged in a good cry. The next
day, she had gotten out and gone back into town to shop.

Her first stop had been a boutique where she'd found
the most gorgeous pair of sandals. Deciding that she
hadn't treated herself to a day of beauty in a while, she'd
visited a spa. A couple of hours later, with several new
beach outfits, new sandals, a pedicure and manicured
nails, she had returned to the beach house feeling a
whole lot better. Pain and anger were no longer at war
inside of her. She had reached the conclusion that no
man would ever take her joy.

She'd also faced a few realities. It seemed her dream
of love, marriage and family was just that—a dream.
Some dreams weren't meant for everyone. Zane had
taught her that lesson. She couldn't put her love and
trust in a man who didn't deserve it, a man who wasn't
capable of loving, a man who couldn't make her happy.
She wanted a man who simply adored her—the way she

would adore him—a man who would love her, a man who wanted the same things she wanted, not because she wanted them but because *they* wanted them.

She'd meant what she'd told Megan. She appreciated Zane for making her realize just how naive she had been. She thought she had taken off the rose-colored glasses the last time she'd left Denver, but this time not only had she taken them off she'd tossed them into the sea. The next man she dated would have to work hard for her affections.

At that moment, she doubted she would ever fall in love again. She'd tried and lost her heart, and now it was time for her to get out of the game.

Zane turned over in bed and glanced at the clock. It was two in the morning. Sitting up, he ran a frustrated hand across his face. Once the haze of his anger over Channing's engagement deception had shifted away, all he could see every time he closed his eyes was her stricken face. It hit him right below the gut each and every time he thought about hurting her.

Unable to sleep, he eased out of bed and went downstairs for a cold drink of water. However, when he opened the refrigerator it was a bottle of beer that he pulled out instead. Leaning against the countertop, he twisted off the bottle cap and took a huge swig, liking the feel of the liquid moving past his throat to hit solidly in his stomach.

He had built this house seven years ago, but this was the first time he'd realized just how lonely it was. His siblings and cousins visited often—and Bailey too much—but he never allowed women to consider his place as their home.

Except for Channing.

He had surprised even himself when he'd given her a key, but he had never questioned why he'd done so. All he'd known was those days when he would arrive home after working with the horses all day and see her car parked in his yard, sensations he couldn't describe tugged at his chest. His mood would brighten as soon as he opened the door and saw her, and he would sweep her up in his arms and kiss her like his entire life depended on it.

He could remember the last time she'd sat at his kitchen table. It had been one morning after she'd spent the night and had awakened early to prepare breakfast for the both of them. They had eaten together, and it had been enjoyable, as usual. But it had been that same morning when Channing had come out and asked where their relationship was headed.

The question had annoyed him because he'd known she was about to bring up something he didn't want to discuss. He had told her he didn't love her and that nothing had changed. Afterward, he had quickly left for work, not wanting to stick around to see how she handled his response. A few weeks later, she had dropped the bomb that she was leaving town. Her decision to leave Denver had made him bitter. He hadn't even bothered to attend the going-away party Megan had thrown for her.

Taking another huge swig of his beer, he pushed away from the counter and walked over to the window to look out in brooding silence. Most people were in bed asleep, but here he was, right where he had been for the past three days, enduring sleepless nights due to a woman he should have gotten over two years ago. She was the only woman who could make emotions tug at him…like they were doing now. In fact, they weren't just tugging; they were eating away at him big-time.

He was still on Megan's and Bailey's bad sides. That much had been evident at tonight's chow-down. His sisters-in-law and his cousins' wives were sending him seething looks, as well. Even Gemma had called him from Australia to give him a blistering earful, saying, *"How could you hurt Channing again, Zane? She is way too good for you. She is liked and well respected by all who know her, and she has a heart of gold. But that isn't enough for you, is it? Any other man would have appreciated the beautiful and heartwarming person that she is. One day you're going to realize just what you lost!"*

Zane released a sigh of pure disgust with himself. While shaving this morning, he had looked himself in the mirror and hadn't liked the person staring back at him. Everyone who had been on him for the past few days was right. Channing deserved a better man than him. She deserved the right to find a man who could love her, make her happy and give her the marriage and family she wanted. She deserved a man who would cherish her, who would show her every day how much she was adored and how proud he would be to have her at his side. Somewhere, that man was out there. The thought made Zane's gut clench. He would rather cut off his arm than lose Channing to another man.

He froze, stunned by what he was thinking. What man would willingly lose a limb for a woman he didn't love? Zane's throat suddenly went dry, and he tilted the beer bottle up to his mouth, quickly chugging down what was left.

It was then that Rico's words came back to haunt him… *I knew I loved your sister when I realized I couldn't live a single day without her.*

Zane drew in a deep breath. He could finally admit that he felt things for Channing that he'd never felt for another woman. He didn't want to let her out of his life. In other words…he couldn't imagine living a single day without her. His heart began pounding in his chest when he knew immediately what that meant.

"Ah, hell," he muttered to himself, glancing down at his empty beer bottle. "That means you've fallen for her, man. And you've fallen hard."

Everything suddenly made sense. Why he'd felt so down in the dumps after she left Denver for Atlanta and why every woman he'd dated after her seemed lacking. It also answered the question of why the thought of her being with another man constantly ate at him. More importantly, it explained why he'd kept that locked box under his bed for two years, unable to let go.

For the first time in his life, Zane Westmoreland loved a woman.

"Hello, Gramma, this is Channing."

"Hi, sweetie. I hope you got to the beach house all right and you're getting settled."

"Yes, I've been here for three days now, and I'm starting to unwind. I needed a break," Channing said, pushing hair back from her face.

"Yes, a break from work is always nice," Adele Hastings said.

Channing glanced out the kitchen window. She had gotten up early to go jogging on the beach. Then she'd returned, showered and prepared breakfast, which she'd enjoyed while catching up on the news on television. The meteorologist had reported a heat wave that was spreading all the way up to New England. This prompted her to check on her grandparents since they liked spending time outdoors. Her parents, who lived within five miles of her grandparents, would usually check on them but they had left last week for a two-week cruise to Hawaii, leaving out of San Diego after visiting with her brother.

"You and Gramps okay? I heard about the heat wave."

"We're fine, but what about you?"

She knew her grandmother was someone she could always talk to, and she felt blessed to have two confidantes, her mother and grandmother. "I'm through with men, Gramma," she said honestly.

There was a pause at the other end of the line, and then Adele asked, "Are you?"

"Yes. You love them, and they don't love you back. And then there are those who claim they do but don't know the meaning of the word—like Emmitt."

Why she had brought up Emmitt Sawyer she would never know. Emmitt had been part of her college days. The first guy she'd ever slept with and the first guy she'd given her heart to. She'd thought he loved her; he'd even told her so a number of times. She'd believed him and had taken him home on spring break to meet the family. Then, at the start of their junior year, when they'd been dating for almost a year, she'd discovered he'd been messing around with a girl who worked as a waitress at some café in town…the entire time he'd been spewing words of love to Channing.

She had returned home brokenhearted. It had been her mother and grandmother who'd convinced her that not all men abused a woman's love. There were men out there who would cherish it. It had taken her five years before she'd put her heart on the line again for Zane.

She had moved from a man who told her he loved her

all the time to a man who didn't hesitate to let her know he didn't love her at all. Both had been heartbreakers.

"So you think men are the problem, Channing?"

Her grandmother's question sliced into her thoughts. "No, I'm the problem. I expect too much and trust too soon. So I'm quitting men."

"Um, that sounds interesting," Adele said calmly.

Channing scowled. "Men aren't good for anything but sex." She suddenly sucked in a quick breath when she remembered who she was talking to.

She could hear her grandmother's chuckle on the other end of the phone. "I'll remember to tell your grandfather that."

Channing dropped down into a kitchen chair. "Oh, Gramma. Gramps is like Dad. They are the greatest. They just don't make men like that anymore."

"Don't they?"

"I thought they did, but now I'm not sure. I'm tired of getting my heart broken. I'm locking up my heart and throwing away the key."

"Are you sure you want to do that, sweetie?"

No, but she felt she didn't have a choice. Like she'd told her grandmother, the problem wasn't with the men but with her. She was the one who had to make changes in the way she thought about love. She could see now that her problem was that she took relationships too seriously because she'd always had an agenda. Maybe it was time to loosen the shackles and be set free. Live a little and have fun.

"Channing?"

She blinked upon realizing she hadn't answered her grandmother's question. "Yes, Gramma, that's what I want to do. That's what I'm going to do."

Knowing she needed to get off the phone before her

grandmother tried to talk her into giving men another chance, Channing stood up. "I need to get dressed. I'm going to spend the day on the beach."

"Oh, all right. If you want to talk again, I'm here."

Channing tightened the belt on her robe. She had the best grandmother in the whole wide world. "Thanks, and I love you."

"I love you back."

Zane felt tired and drained. He didn't have to be told he wasn't pulling his share of the work today. It disgusted him even more when Derringer and Jason gave him pathetic gazes.

When they took a break for lunch, Jason left to meet his wife, Bella. They were adding more rooms to her grandfather's home, which they'd turned into a bed-and-breakfast, and they were meeting with the contractors.

Zane glanced over at Derringer as they sat across from each other outside at a picnic table eating the sandwiches and drinking the tea Derringer's wife, Lucia, had made for them. "You're quiet," Zane said.

Derringer met Zane's gaze. "I was just thinking. I couldn't sleep last night and woke up around two. After checking on the baby, I went downstairs to get something to drink."

Zane nodded. That was what he'd been doing around that time.

"Do you know what happened when I walked into my kitchen, Zane?"

Zane frowned. "No."

"I swear I could smell gingerbread."

Zane didn't say anything. He didn't have to. All he had to do was remember the days when he and his siblings would wake up to the aroma of gingerbread. Their mother loved to bake, and gingerbread cookies were her favorite as well as theirs.

"Then it hit me that it's been almost twenty years, but damn it, I still miss Mom like yesterday," Derringer said, obviously trying to keep the pain from his voice. "Both her and Dad...but especially Mom. She had a way of making all our wrongs right."

Zane had to agree. Their mother had been special, and Susan Westmoreland had fostered a close relationship with all her children. He'd been in his late teens when his parents had died—in his second year of college. He recalled when he'd been around sixteen. At the peak of his dating years in high school, he'd thought he was a Casanova, the school's stud. His mother would warn him about breaking some girl's heart and claimed that if he wasn't careful someday a girl would come along and break his.

"I've been thinking of her a lot lately, too," Zane confessed. "I often wonder how different things would be if that plane hadn't crashed. Dillon would be retiring from the NBA about now, and Ramsey would have come out of college to become a sheep rancher and not have gone to work at Blue Ridge. And," he added with a smile, "we wouldn't have had the trouble that we did out of the twins, Bane and Bailey. The first time Bailey said a curse word around Mom her ass would have been grass."

"Yeah." Derringer chuckled. "Mom didn't play. But she also had a soft heart. All the neighbors loved her and Aunt Clarisse."

Zane had a feeling his mother would have liked the spouses her sons and daughters had married. Ramsey was happy with Chloe, Derringer was head over heels in love with Lucia and both Gemma and Megan had married good men who worshipped the ground they walked on. He drew in a deep breath, suddenly convinced his mother would have loved Channing, as well.

Neither Derringer nor Zane said anything for a minute, and then Zane asked, "When did you know you loved Lucia?"

If Derringer found the question odd, he didn't say. Instead, he took a sip of his iced tea. "First of all, I fought it like hell. The reason I never let any woman get close to me was because the very thought of falling in love and getting attached to someone sent chills up my spine. The thought of losing them the way we lost our folks and Uncle Adam and Aunt Clarisse was unacceptable to me. I had this fear of loving Lucia and then losing her the way we lost Mom."

Zane studied his brother. He wondered if Derringer knew that Zane had similar fears. "How did you overcome them? Those fears."

"By realizing that life is full of risks. Things happen. I couldn't live my life waiting for something bad to come my way. Then I decided that nothing, especially not my fears, weighed more heavily than my desire to be with Lucia, to build a life with her and make a family. That's when I admitted to myself that I cared more for her than for any other woman before, that I loved her. And when a man loves a woman he will move heaven and hell, if necessary, to make her the most important person in his life, regardless of the risks. She is worth the risk. She becomes your life."

Zane didn't say anything as he continued to sip his tea. He knew in his heart that Channing was worth the risk. She was a vital part of his life, but up to now he'd been too afraid to admit it.

The thought of loving a woman was scary as hell,

but what was even scarier was the possibility that he'd lost her and might not ever see her again. Or the thought that wherever she was she hated his guts.

"Can I ask you something, Zane?"

Zane glanced over at his brother. "Yes."

"Do you love Channing?"

Zane sucked in a quick breath at his brother's question, but then only moments later he answered by saying, "I believe I do."

Derringer shook his head. "That's not good enough. You need to know for certain. You owe it to yourself, as well as to her, to know what your true feelings are. Do you know what I think, Zane?"

Zane poured out the rest of his tea. "No, what do you think, Derringer?"

"You're afraid to admit to falling in love for the same reason I was. Losing people you love is hard. But you need to weigh all the options. Think of all the things that might happen and those that might not. Then ask yourself if spending time with Channing every day for the rest of your life is worth the risks."

Derringer glanced at his watch when he saw Jason returning. "I guess it's time for us to get back to work."

Zane found it hard to focus on work without thoughts of Channing and what his brother had said consuming his mind. For years, his brothers and cousins had considered him the know-it-all where women were concerned, and he did know a lot. But the one thing he *didn't* know was how to love and appreciate the one woman who should have mattered. The one woman who was meant for him.

Channing was meant for him. He could see that now.

A few hours later, telling Derringer and Jason that he needed to leave for a while, Zane got in his truck and drove over to Megan's Meadows at breakneck speed. He figured his sister was still at work and was glad it was Rico who opened the door. Before Rico could say anything, Zane spoke up and said, "I want to know where Channing is."

At the frown that settled on Rico's face, Zane held up his hand. "I love her, man."

Rico studied Zane, and then he nodded slowly.

"I figured you would come to your senses sooner or later. But be prepared. Love or no love, I don't think she's going to make things easy for you. Personally, I wouldn't."

Zane wasn't surprised by that. "Yes, but there's no way I'm not going to try."

Six

One of Channing's favorite spots in her grandmother's beach house was the window seat. She remembered when her grandfather had knocked down the wall to build it—a huge bay window with a padded seat long enough to stretch out on. One night in her teen years she'd even slept here. She'd woken up staring out at the ocean.

So here she sat with her legs stretched out in front of her while reading a book. The story had held her attention for the past two days, and she planned to finish it later tonight. After reaching a good stopping place, she placed her book aside, stood to stretch and decided to go to the kitchen to get something to drink.

Her brother hadn't called, which meant her grandparents hadn't mentioned anything to him and she appreciated that. The last thing she needed was for Juan to call wanting to know why she wasn't in Denver when she'd told him she would be there awhile. He was five years older and could be overprotective at times.

Although neither her parents nor Juan had met Zane, she had mentioned him on a number of occasions, so there was no doubt in her mind that they were aware she'd fallen in love. Just like there was no doubt in her mind that they knew the relationship had ended. No one had asked, but her family was astute enough to know her decision to leave Denver two years ago had something to do with Zane.

She was heading back to her window seat with a cold glass of lemonade when there was a knock at the door. She smiled, figuring it was the six-year-old girl she'd met yesterday on the beach. The youngster, Sandy Farmer, was an absolute doll. She and her parents and her adorable nine-month-old baby brother had rented the beach house next door for the entire summer. The parents were probably in their early thirties, and it was easy to see that they were in love.

Jennifer Farmer had let Channing hold her son, and the moment she had held the baby in her arms she recalled a time when she'd dreamed of marrying Zane and having his child. But then, in that same dream, she had fooled herself into thinking he loved her. The Farmer family was beautiful, and seeing them together made Channing realize just what she might never have.

But she'd decided not to take men or relationships seriously, she reminded herself, as she placed the glass of lemonade on the table and moved toward the door. Sandy had paid her a visit a few hours ago to see if Channing wanted to build sand castles on the beach.

Ready to tell Sandy she couldn't go out on the beach with her just yet, she opened the door.

"Hello, Channing."

* * *

From Channing's expression, Zane knew he was the last person she'd expected to see. She looked amazing with bare feet and wearing a short denim skirt and a lavender T-shirt. While she was still standing in the doorway, stunned, he figured he would ease inside before the shock wore off.

When he closed the door behind him, shock was replaced with anger. "Hey, wait a minute! I didn't invite you in. What are you doing here, Zane?"

"I came to apologize, Channing," he said, leaning back against the closed door. "The reason I did what I did that night at McKays was because I thought you were engaged to Hammond, and I didn't want to see you get hurt."

She gaped at him. "You didn't want to see me hurt? So seducing me just for the hell of it, to prove a point, wasn't going to hurt me?"

Zane crossed his arms over his chest. "I did not seduce you for the hell of it, Channing. I did it to make sure you would break off your engagement. At the time, I thought it was a good idea. Hammond was screwing around on you. How was I to know the two of you weren't really engaged?"

Channing clenched her jaw before saying. "That's beside the point! How Mack was treating me wasn't any of your business."

"The hell it wasn't. Was I supposed to stand around and let him mess with you?"

She looked livid. "Yes, that's precisely what you were supposed to do. It wasn't your business, Zane. *I'm* not your business. You didn't want me, remember? Who I became involved with after leaving Denver wasn't your concern. You can't have it both ways. You don't love me yet you didn't think twice about sabotaging what, for all you knew, was my happiness with another man."

Zane shook his head at their senseless argument. "I do love you."

Channing froze. And then seconds later, when he leaned in closer, she blinked. When he grasped her chin to tilt her face up to his, the only thing she seemed able to do was stare up at him. Did he really think she would believe that he loved her after all the times he'd denied it? No, Zane didn't love her. He just didn't want anyone else to have her. Hadn't he all but told her that very thing at McKays?

"I'm sorry I made you mad at me, but I'm here now, and everything is going to be fine, baby. You'll see."

Before she could respond, he licked his tongue across her lips slowly with deliberate strokes. He toyed with her mouth by sliding his tongue in and out between her parted lips. Her traitorous body let out a moan.

There were some things a woman couldn't get over, and that was how skilled a man could be at seduction. Zane was an ace. He could kiss the panties off a woman, and she of all people should know since he'd proved that skill on her a number of times.

Moments later, he lifted his head from her mouth, and she could hear his heavy breathing. But what made her breath catch were the dark brown eyes fixed on hers. He was staring at her in a way that made her insides melt.

"I want you," he whispered huskily against her lips.

Channing tried to ignore how quickly he had gone from loving her to wanting her. It was obvious Zane Westmoreland didn't know the difference between love and lust. And, for now, she didn't want to know, either. There was no denying she wanted him, and as long as she knew that love wasn't a part of the equation there was no reason she couldn't enjoy him.

Hadn't she told her grandmother a few days ago she was locking up her heart and throwing away the key? Zane showing up like this didn't change a thing. As far as she was concerned, his declaration of love was nothing but words. Words she refused to believe in.

"Channing, say you want me, too," he said throatily, holding her gaze with his dark eyes.

What he was asking of her was easy. "I want you, too, Zane."

A smile touched his face, and he drew her closer, putting his hands on her rounded bottom, cupping her in a way that placed an arch in her back and made her press tight to his middle.

She felt him, the heavy bulge of his erection through his jeans. Even through the denim she could feel him throbbing. She wrapped her arms around his neck, and they stared at each other as sexual heat surrounded them, stimulating them, charging the air. Erotic tension vibrated between them, and a gigantic craving rushed blood through her veins.

Then, soundlessly, he lowered his mouth back down to hers.

Zane felt his world rocking the moment their mouths locked. Tongues touched, entwined, twirled with a hunger that tugged mercilessly at his groin. Damn, he had missed this. He had lain in bed plenty of nights remembering. Channing had a mouth that was made to be kissed, and he had taken great joy in doing so. She had a taste that was unique, and his tongue was greedy ready to make up for lost time.

She was kissing him back, tangling her tongue with

his in a heated duel, a sensuous motion that made his erection throb harder. There had never been a time when she hadn't met him on a primal level. There had never been a time when she hadn't both fueled and satisfied a need within him. Even now, his stomach muscles quivered as raw desire took control of him.

He shifted his stance so the apex of her thighs made better contact with his erection. He wanted her to feel it, to know what she was doing to him, to know just how much he wanted her.

Zane deepened the kiss, and the moan that came from deep within Channing's throat told him all he needed to know. He wouldn't have to grovel as he'd thought he would have to do. Like he'd been prepared to do. Like him, she was ready for them to move into the future together.

He pulled his mouth from hers and stared down into eyes glazed over in passion. How could he not have known he loved her? How could he have missed the truth when all signs pointed to those emotions he hadn't wanted to acknowledge? She had been the one even when he'd convinced himself that she was not.

He loved her. He needed her. And he never intended to let her go again. Derringer was right. The thought of not having Channing in his life far outweighed the fear of losing her to some tragic event.

Filled with love to a depth that was mind-boggling, he cupped her face in his hands. She looked absolutely beautiful, staring up at him with hazel eyes. Suddenly, something clenched in his gut. He saw desire in her eyes, but where was the vibrancy that was always there when she looked at him? He recalled seeing it that night at McKays. Perplexed as to why he would imagine such a thing, he asked softly, "You okay?"

She nodded. "Yes, why wouldn't I be?"

Good question. Zane grew thoughtful. But before he could dwell on her response any further, Channing placed her hands on his shoulders. At her touch, his heart pounded furiously in his chest. Needing to have his mouth connected to hers once again, he leaned down and feasted on it like a desperate man. The only times he'd ever been this hot for a woman had always been with Channing.

He moaned deep in his throat when he felt her hips grind against his hard length, sending rapid sensations rippling through him. The sensual pull between them was too strong, more overpowering than ever before, and he needed her now.

She released a startled gasp when he swept her off her feet and into his arms. Glancing down at her, he asked, "Where's the bedroom?"

"Straight ahead on your right."

He walked at a brisk pace, feeling the urgency in every step. When they reached the bedroom, he placed her on her feet beside the bed. "Do you have any idea how I feel?" he asked, letting his fingers tenderly stroke the side of her face.

"No."

Zane paused. She'd given him a quick and simple answer. "Then let me show you."

The one thing he'd always enjoyed during their time together was his ability to pleasure Channing. Her body would respond to him in the most sensuous ways. She loved the taste and feel of him as much as he did her.

He murmured gently, telling her in plain terms just what he planned to do to her. He heard how breathless she became with every explicit detail.

He removed several condom packets from his wal-

let and tossed them on the bed. Then, without wasting
any time, he quickly shed his shoes and socks before
yanking his shirt from his jeans and removing the rest
of his clothing.

"Now for you to join me," he said, laving his tongue
across her jaw. He then stripped her of her T-shirt, pulling it over her head and tossing it aside. He cupped her
breasts through her lace bra, and his entire body felt
an electrical charge. Then, with a flick of his wrist, the
front clasp was undone and gorgeous twin globes were
free, making his mouth water with heated male appreciation as he gazed at them.

"Beautiful," he murmured, heat stirring in his gut.
Her breasts were perfectly shaped, enticing to the eyes
and delicious to the mouth. Lowering his head, he bur-
ied his face between them and inhaled the luscious scent
of her flesh.

Breathing thickly, Zane's mouth latched onto a swollen nipple and licked it with the tip of his tongue before
sucking greedily. He felt and heard her body's response
when she shivered and moaned, which triggered a similar reaction in him. Blood pulsed through the veins of
his engorged shaft, making it ache that much more.

A thrill of intense pleasure ripped through Channing, and she held Zane's head to her breasts as his
mouth had its way with them. Her nipples throbbed
while being devoured by his tongue, and her belly quivered with intense arousal that moved lower, to the apex
of her thighs. It was only a matter of time before he
took note and gave her the kind of attention that only
he could give.

Moments later, he lifted his head and inhaled deeply.
She watched how his nostrils flared as they picked up

her scent. In anticipation of his next move, thunderbolts of pleasure consumed her.

"I need to get inside you, bad," he said softly, reaching behind her to ease down the back zipper of her skirt. He gave it a little tug, and the denim slid down her thighs to pool at her bare feet. Her heart pounded furiously in her chest when he lowered to bended knees and removed her panties, easing them down her legs.

Instead of standing back up, he remained on his knees. He touched the curly hair covering her femininity. His fingers slid back and forth through the curls before parting her folds and easing inside of her.

Desire shifted into an urgency that Channing felt all the way through her bones. And when he added another finger and began working inside of her, stroking her with mindless precision, she threw her head back and moaned. She wasn't just wet; she was soaked—exactly the way Zane liked.

"I can't wait to taste you again," he whispered, his voice reaching her just moments before his tongue slid inside of her. Then, with his ardently skillful and proficient mouth, he licked, sucked and nibbled her right into an explosion.

But he didn't let up. All through her orgasm, he swirled his tongue inside of her, lapping her greedily as he held on to her with his mouth.

She cried out, screaming his name while bucking her hips, holding on to his firm, broad shoulders. She thought the same thing now that she'd thought the first time he had taken her this way. Zane Westmoreland's tongue should be outlawed and his fingers shackled.

It was only when the last spasm had left her body that he got to his feet, cupped her face in his hands and held her gaze. "I love you."

Channing's mind blocked out his words. She didn't want to hear them because they weren't true. He didn't love her; he loved this. He wasn't in love with her; he was in lust with her.

He kissed her, and she tasted herself on his lips while his engorged length pressed hard against her stomach. Licking her lips, she pushed Zane down on the bed with the intention of savoring every inch of him. It had been two years, and she'd missed his taste.

He lay flat on his back as she eased over him, using her tongue to lick all the way from his ankles to where his shaft lay thick and swollen in a dense bed of curly hair. She used her fingers to stroke him before lowering her lips to his throbbing erection.

As soon as her mouth took him in, he let out a guttural groan. The sound sent heat surging through her. Her mouth tortured him, and she enjoyed the feel of him pulsating against her lips. Blood raced through her body when she felt him swell even more. He jerked, bucked and arched off the bed, but she refused to let go. This was what she wanted, what she craved, what she'd missed.

"Channing!"

Her mouth stayed locked on him even when he screamed out her name and his release flooded her mouth. She felt his hands in her hair, trying to pull her mouth away, but she refused to let go. His taste was setting her entire body on fire, preparing her for what was coming next.

She slowly eased her mouth off him, and before she could catch her breath, he had pulled her up and flipped her gently onto her back. Parting her legs with his knees, he looked down at her before reaching for one of the condoms he'd tossed on the bed earlier. He opened the packet with his teeth and quickly sheathed himself.

"I need this," he whispered before easing into her. He then thrust hard, and she wrapped her legs around him. He rode her, moving in and out, using powerful strokes, sensuous thrusts and a steady pace that had heat drumming through her at every angle.

The room filled with the scent of hot, sweaty bodies. Hard, gritty sex. And Zane was relentless. She responded by lifting her body to meet his downward spiral over and over again.

And then she went crashing over the edge, taking him with her. His body continued the steady strokes until the last remnants of climax had left her body, leaving her totally drained. She was convinced that what they'd shared today felt different from all those other times. She'd never experienced anything like it.

Moments later, Zane slowly pulled out of her and then eased out of the bed to go to the bathroom. When he returned, Channing lay stretched across the bed with her arms thrown over her eyes, pulling in deep breaths.

She lowered her arms so she could look up at him. He had put on his jeans but not his shirt. The woman in her couldn't help but appreciate his muscular chest. When he made a move to sit on the edge of the bed, she said, "You need to leave, Zane."

His brows rose in surprise. "Leave?"

"Yes. I enjoyed the sex as much as you did. We both got what we wanted, so there's no reason for you to stick around."

A dark frown settled on his face. "What are you talking about?"

"I'm talking about the reason you came here."

"I told you why I came. I wanted to apologize and to tell you I love you."

She shook her head as she eased out of bed and began

putting on her clothes. She glanced over at him as she tossed her hair aside to slide her T-shirt back over her head. "I don't believe you."

He watched her every move. "What don't you believe?"

She eased her skirt up over her hips. "That you love me."

Zane was taken aback by what she said. "And why don't you believe me?"

"Because," she said, pulling her hair back and fastening it with a clip. "If you tell someone something often enough, eventually they'll get smart and believe it. You didn't love me a few days ago. I got that admission from your own lips. So why on earth would I believe that you love me now, Zane?"

Seven

Zane stood there with his gaze fixed on Channing. He could not believe she was questioning what he'd told her. The first time he'd ever admitted his love for a woman and she didn't believe him? What kind of crap was that?

Somewhere in the back of his mind, he could hear Bailey gloating. *"The kind of crap you got yourself into."*

Drawing in a frustrated breath, he said, "The reason you should believe me is because I don't have a reason to lie about anything like that."

She gave a short laugh. "Sure you do. You've got it in your mind that nobody can have me but you."

He took it as an affront at what she said. "I don't think that!"

"Don't you?" Her eyes turned stormy. "Did you not seduce me in McKays to prove a point?"

"Yes, but I—"

"Doesn't matter," she said, interrupting. "You've explained yourself. You came to apologize, and you have. But please don't get love confused with lust, Zane. You can never love a woman. I get it."

No, she didn't get it. How could a man tell a woman he loved her and she not believe him? He drew in a deep breath when the answer slapped him in the face. Easily, if it was the same man who'd told her over and over that he didn't love her.

They stood there, eyes locked, while seconds ticked by. He needed her to understand. "I was afraid to love you until now."

Her brows rose. "Afraid? Please. Certainly you can do better than that. Zane Westmoreland isn't afraid of anything."

Boy, was she wrong. He rubbed his hand down his face in frustration. "Look, Channing—"

"No, you look," she said, her tone hardening as she tossed him his shirt. "You might not know what love is, but I do. I loved you, but you couldn't love me back. You *wouldn't* love me back. So I left Denver, and I stayed away for two years. Two years, Zane. And you didn't so much as pick up a phone to see how I was doing."

Her heart twisted, remembering the nights when she first got to Atlanta when, for some stupid reason, she actually thought he would come after her. She thought that he'd realize he loved her, he couldn't live without her and he would show up one day with a confession of his feelings. She had been so wrong, and when she'd finally accepted that Zane truly didn't give a damn about her, she'd tried moving on.

"I wanted to," Zane said and immediately knew it sounded lame.

Evidently she thought so, too. He could tell when he

saw fire flaring in her eyes. "You wanted to? The Zane who does whatever he wants to do *wanted* to call me and couldn't? Why?" She held up her hand before he could answer. "That's right, you were afraid," she said, mocking his earlier statement. She crossed her arms over her chest. "And just what were you were afraid of, Zane? Were you scared that I would pressure you into marrying me?"

Zane knew women, and he knew you couldn't make them see reason when they believed there was none. And you definitely couldn't out-talk one who thought she had a case to make.

"You're upset, Channing. Maybe we should continue this conversation tomorrow."

"Don't count on it. Why don't you just head back to Denver? After that to-prove-a-point stunt you pulled in McKays, I don't want you around."

A dark scowl covered his face. "What do you call what we just did in this bed, Channing? We made love."

She gave him a smirking look, one like he'd never gotten from her before. "No, we didn't make love. We had sex. I'm sure you're very familiar with the act."

"Damn it, Channing. I could never have just sex with you!" he stormed.

"Then let me inform you that you just did." She slid her feet into a pair of flat shoes. "Put your shirt on so I can walk you to the door."

A nerve ticked in Zane's jaw. Not only did she think so little of what they'd just shared but she was kicking him out! He opened his mouth to say a few words, but when he saw tears welling in her eyes he muttered a curse under his breath instead. Tears she was fighting like hell for him not to see. At that moment, he was

filled with remorse that he had hurt the one woman he
should have protected from all harm.

"Channing, I do love—"

"No," she lashed out, halting his words in midsen-
tence. "Just leave, Zane. Please, just leave."

Feeling helpless on one hand and like a total ass on
the other, Zane pushed out a deep breath and put on his
shirt. He kept his gaze on Channing. "You're wrong
about me, Channing, and I intend to prove it."

"Don't waste your time trying to prove another point,
Zane. I've taken off the rose-colored glasses and tossed
them away. I did the same thing with the key to my
heart."

He shoved his hands into his pockets, refusing to go
down in defeat. "Then I guess my job is to find both
and return them."

"Like I said, don't waste your time." She tossed the
words over her shoulder as she led him out of the room
to the door.

Zane's gut tightened when he heard Channing's door
slam shut behind him. He paused when he reached the
rental car. He had a mind to go right back up to her
door and demand that she see reason, demand that she
believe him.

Demand? Hell, he of all people should know you
couldn't demand anything from a woman—especially
one who felt she'd been wronged. He swallowed a deep
lump in his throat at the realization that she *had* been
wronged. So far he hadn't handled anything right with
Channing. Feeling totally disgusted with himself, he
opened the car door and slid inside, snapping the seat
belt in place.

His hands gripped the steering wheel as he looked

over his shoulder before backing out of her yard. He was in one hell of a mess and he—Zane Westmoreland who was considered the expert on any issues dealing with women—didn't know what he needed to do to fix things.

He'd figured showing up and confessing his love would do it. He'd been dead wrong. A part of him was angry that she actually thought he would lie about something like that. Hell, he took those three words seriously. She'd suggested that he might be getting love confused with lust. Did she not think he knew the difference? Hell, he'd lusted after women since puberty. But he'd never felt the need to chase behind one and pour out his heart and soul.

The nerve of her, questioning his words of love. It was almost enough to make him want to drive back to the airport and catch the next plane to Denver. He didn't need this.

But he did need her. And regardless of what she thought, he did love her.

When he came to a stop at a traffic light, Zane closed his eyes and conjured up the image he'd seen when she'd opened the door for him to leave. The look on her face was the same one he'd see when he'd broken things off with other women. But he'd never seen that look on her.

Some women just couldn't accept, for whatever reason, that their relationship had come to the end. Seeing that look had never bothered him before because he'd felt it was the woman's problem and not his. Unfortunately, he couldn't think that way with Channing because he loved her. It *was* his problem.

He opened his eyes when a car behind him honked, letting him know the traffic light had changed. Moments later, he made a right at the intersection that would take him to one of the many hotels in the area. If Channing thought she'd gotten rid of him then she was sadly mistaken.

It was a beautiful day in July, and the ocean looked magnificent. As he drove along the beach's scenic route, his gaze took in the beautiful landscape. He'd been to Virginia before, with Derringer and Jason, when they met with a rancher in Richmond who'd been interested in purchasing a number of their horses.

As he was driving, his cell phone rang. Thinking it might be Channing calling to let him know she did believe his confession of love after all, his heart pounded in his chest. Entering the hotel's parking lot, he brought his car to a stop in one of the spaces and quickly shifted to pull his cell phone out of his pocket. He frowned when he saw the caller was not Channing but his cousin Canyon.

"What's up, Canyon?"

"Where the hell are you, Zane? I dropped by the Hideout last night and again this morning, and it looks like a ghost town. I asked Derringer and Jason when I saw you weren't working with the horses today. They both had locked lips for some reason."

Good for them, Zane thought, turning off the car's ignition. He'd told Derringer and Jason not to mention where he'd gone unless an emergency came up. The last thing he wanted was for Megan to get wind of the fact that he'd come after Channing. He didn't want her to try and sabotage things for him. He'd gotten Rico's word that he wouldn't mention it to Megan for a few days, to give Zane time to make his case with Channing.

Zane figured Canyon must be hunting him down due to some woman issue. He was tempted to tell Canyon that he had his own problems to deal with. "I'm out of town on business, Canyon." In a way, that was true. Channing *was* his business.

"Well, I need to talk to you about something."

Zane rolled his eyes. "Something or someone?"

"Someone. I told you Keisha Ashford was back in town."

Keisha was a woman his cousin had been involved with a few years ago. "Yes, you mentioned she'd returned and had gotten rehired at that law firm in town."

"Well, I've been trying to get her to talk to me so we can clear up what drove us apart, but she won't give me the time of day."

Welcome to the club, Zane thought. "And?"

"And I don't understand how she could have thought I betrayed her with another woman."

Zane gritted his teeth. He understood Canyon's dilemma since he couldn't understand why Channing would think he didn't love her. "Well, she did walk in on you and—"

"Bonita and I hadn't done anything," Canyon said.

"Yes, but I can understand why Keisha had a hard time believing that since Bonita Simpkins was naked and all…and if I recall the story, so were you."

"I was wearing a towel because I had just taken a shower."

"Oh." He wondered if Canyon fully realized just how damaging that must have looked. "Let me ask you this," Zane said. "When the two of you were together did you ever tell Keisha how you felt about her?"

"Of course I did. I don't have commitment issues like you."

Zane frowned. "What do you mean by that?"

"What I mean is that I happen not to see falling in love as some sort of a curse. My parents, as well as yours, had good marriages. Solid and strong. That's the reason the thought of a wife and kids never threw me into a state of panic like it did you."

Zane took offense. "It never threw me into a state of panic. I just wasn't ready to settle down."

"And you won't ever be."

Zane's frown deepened. "What if I told you that I had fallen in love?"

Canyon laughed. "Then I would tell you to go tell that lie to somebody else. You're incapable of falling in love. Now back to Keisha."

Zane took the phone from his ear and stared at it. If his own kin didn't believe he was capable of falling in love, then how could he expect Channing to believe it?

He put the phone back to his ear to hear Canyon rambling. His cousin was thirty-two and an attorney at the family firm. He'd started out as a medical student at Howard University and after the second year decided becoming a doctor wasn't for him. He'd switched to Howard's School of Law instead. Now he worked as an attorney at Blue Ridge. "Riley said I should make peace with her," Canyon said.

"And?"

"I tried, but she refuses to give me the time of day. I don't even know where she lives, man. She refuses to tell me. And the few times I've run into her, she acted secretive. Like she's hiding something."

Zane drew in a deep breath. "So exactly what do you want from me, Canyon?"

"You're the expert on women. What do you think I should do?"

Zane snorted. Yeah, he was an expert all right. An expert who couldn't handle his own damn business. "First of all, she's probably not acting secretive, Canyon. She's probably being coy. Keisha's sizing you up to see if you can be trusted again. Trust is important to a woman." *So is being told she's loved,* Zane thought.

"I didn't betray her," Canyon blasted.

"Doesn't matter. She thinks she caught you red-handed. You're going to have to prove Bonita Simpkins set you up."

"Why should I have to prove anything? She should have trusted me. I didn't do anything wrong, and I'm sick and tired of her treating me like I did. Goodbye, Zane. I'll see you when you get back to Denver. And where are you, anyway? You didn't say."

And he didn't intend to. "Gotta go, Canyon. I've just made it to the hotel."

"Oh, okay. When will you be back?"

Now that was a good question. He intended to stay for as long as it took to convince Channing that he was in love with her. "Not sure, but I'll keep in touch. Talk to you later."

Zane ended the call and decided he needed to come up with a solid plan. He'd gotten himself into this mess, and he would figure a way out of it.

What was this nonsense about them just having sex? Their time in the bedroom had always had more meaning than that. It had never been just sex for him.

He winced upon realizing that he'd never told her that. But somehow Channing had fallen in love with him anyway with the hope that one day he would love her back. Instead, he had looked her right in the eyes and told her—on more than one occasion—that he didn't love her, that he wasn't capable of loving women. And now he expected her to believe otherwise. Today, angry and hurt, she had shown him that things didn't work that way.

He opened the car door, thinking that no matter what it took, he would convince Channing that he did love her.

Whenever she got in a tizzy about anything, Channing had a tendency to cook…and not just a little bit of food. She released a sigh as she glanced around the kitchen at her handiwork. Ignoring the pots and pans stacked sky-high in her kitchen sink, she studied all the containers that littered her table, countertops and island. She had finished everything down to the chocolate chip cookies that had just come out of the oven.

She walked over to the refrigerator to grab a wine cooler, deciding to sit outside on the porch awhile. She'd cooked enough food to last her for the next two and a half weeks. But she couldn't help it. She needed to keep busy, and cooking had always been her solace. This time she'd ended up with spaghetti, two different casseroles, baked chicken, four kinds of veggies, rice, corn on the cob and green beans.

It was more than enough food to share. She immediately thought of the Farmers. There was no reason they couldn't benefit from her madness.

Had it been only a few hours ago that she'd engaged in incredible sex? If the tingling sensation between her legs was anything to go by, she would admit she could use some more. That was what two years without intimacy could do to a woman. She'd always enjoyed sharing a bed with Zane. The man was walking testosterone on legs. And in bed he was simply amazing. Truly unbelievable.

And yet he wanted her to believe that he loved her.
Yeah, right.

Channing shook her head as she opened the door and

sat down on the porch swing. Zane must have forgotten who he was trying to convince. She had been the one, like the others, who'd gotten his spiel when they'd first started dating and the one who'd also heard it plenty of times in between. *I will never love any woman. I don't love you. I'm not capable of falling in love.*

And then he'd stop reiterating it, and she'd made the mistake of thinking she was different. She'd wanted to mean more than the others.

Channing took a deep swallow of her wine cooler, deciding not to rehash the mistakes she'd made with Zane. She was trying so hard to get over him, but after he'd shown up here and made love to her, he'd probably only made things worse. He had stirred up wants and desires she'd convinced herself she didn't have, but what had happened last week in McKays had proved otherwise. She had let him take her on a table in a restaurant for heaven's sake. The only regret she had was that he'd only done it to prove a point.

What if he's telling you the truth about loving you? What if…

Channing pushed the possibility out of her head. There was no way. It was lust, not love. She got it now. She would never be confused again. And hopefully Zane was on his way back to Denver.

Eight

The next morning, Zane pulled up in front of Channing's grandparents' home with a purpose and a plan. He'd never pursued a woman in his life, but giving Channing up wasn't an option. He hadn't gone to bed until he'd come up with this idea. And now he was back with a game changer.

If anyone had presented this problem to him, he would have told them, based on what he knew about women, that actions speak louder than words. Since Channing didn't believe a word he said, it was time to show it.

The next thing he would do was let her think she was in control. Some women enjoyed having the upper hand when a man fell in love with them. They had to see it happening before believing it was real. Especially when it came to a devout bachelor. The woman had to feel she'd succeeded into pushing the man into loving her. When she assumed she'd used her feminine wiles to conquer the man's heart, that made victory so much sweeter.

If that was what was needed, then he was game. And he planned to enjoy every single minute Channing thought she was winning him over, mainly because he would be winning her over, as well. And he knew just how to do it because he knew Channing—her weaknesses and her strengths.

By the time it was over and done, the how of it wouldn't matter because he'd loved her, anyway. And when he was through, there would be no doubt in Channing's mind that she was his woman and he was her man.

Her man.

Where was the shudder he was supposed to feel at being any woman's man? In fact, he felt pretty damn good when he considered the idea. And he also felt good about the fact that Channing still loved him although he was sure she would deny it with her last breath. What had happened yesterday in that bedroom wasn't just about sex like she'd claimed. It had been about making love.

To Channing, passion and love were synonymous, and there had been a lot of passion in that bed yesterday. But he wasn't stupid. Although she might still love him, that love was being held hostage by her mistrust, and he'd have to work hard to release it. More than anything he had to find a way to rekindle that love.

Smiling, Zane swiftly walked up the steps to the porch and glanced at the swing. He'd seen it yesterday but had been too focused on Channing to pay much attention to it. He could see her in the swing. He would be sitting there with her, his arms around her and her head resting on his chest. He'd whisper that he loved her while the motion of the swing rocked them. She would believe him when he said the words. And there would be no doubt in her mind of his sincerity.

He was about to knock on the door when he glanced through her living room window. He paused, angling his head for a better view. When he got it, anger shot through him. A man was moving around Channing's kitchen. What the hell!

A deep scowl covered his face as he moved toward the door. He didn't know what was going on, but he was about to find out.

"Jennifer and I thank you kindly for all this food, Channing."

Channing smiled as she continued packing up the containers. "No problem, Ronald. You're actually doing me a favor. I hadn't meant to cook so much."

Ronald Farmer glanced around the kitchen. "Yes, I would say you did get a bit carried away."

Channing threw back her head and laughed. It was then that she heard the knock at the door. "Would you get the door for me? That's probably Dan Joyner. His grandfather owns the house with the gate down the road. I've known him for years, and he's stopping by to get some of this food, as well."

"Sure."

Zane was about to knock on the door again when it was opened by the man he'd viewed through the window. Dressed in a pair of shorts and a T-shirt, the man was as tall as Zane but with the body of someone who worked out often. The man had the nerve to be smiling.

"How are you doing?" the man greeted with a friendly air. "You're here for the food?"

Zane frowned. "No, I'm not here for any food. I'm

YOUR PARTICIPATION IS REQUESTED!

Dear Reader,

Since you are a lover of romance fiction – we would like to get to know you!

Inside you will find a short Reader's Survey. Sharing your answers with us will help our editorial staff understand who you are and what activities you enjoy.

To thank you for your participation, we would like to send you 2 books and 2 gifts – **ABSOLUTELY FREE!**

Enjoy your gifts with our appreciation,

Pam Powers

SEE INSIDE FOR READER'S SURVEY

For Your Romance Reading Pleasure...

USA TODAY BESTSELLING AUTHOR
BARBARA DUNLOP
MILLIONAIRE IN A STETSON

USA TODAY BESTSELLING AUTHOR
CATHERINE MANN
PLAYING FOR KEEPS

FREE!

We'll send you 2 books and 2 gifts
ABSOLUTELY FREE
just for completing our Reader's Survey!

YOUR READER'S SURVEY
"THANK YOU" FREE GIFTS INCLUDE:
▶ 2 Harlequin Desire® books
▶ 2 lovely surprise gifts

PLEASE FILL IN THE CIRCLES COMPLETELY TO RESPOND

1) What type of fiction books do you enjoy reading? (Check all that apply)
- ○ Suspense/Thrillers   ○ Action/Adventure   ○ Modern-day Romances
- ○ Historical Romance   ○ Humour   ○ Paranormal Romance

2) What attracted you most to the last fiction book you purchased on impulse?
- ○ The Title   ○ The Cover   ○ The Author   ○ The Story

3) What is usually the greatest influencer when you <u>plan</u> to buy a book?
- ○ Advertising   ○ Referral   ○ Book Review

4) How often do you access the internet?
- ○ Daily ○ Weekly ○ Monthly ○ Rarely or never.

5) How many NEW paperback fiction novels have you purchased in the past 3 months?
- ○ 0 - 2   ○ 3 - 6   ○ 7 or more

YES! I have completed the Reader's Survey. Please send me the 2 FREE books and 2 FREE gifts (gifts are worth about $10) for which I qualify. I understand that I am under no obligation to purchase any books, as explained on the back of this card.

225/326 HDL F5GC

FIRST NAME	LAST NAME

ADDRESS

APT.#	CITY

STATE/PROV.	ZIP/POSTAL CODE

✦ HARLEQUIN® READER SERVICE—Here's How It Works:

Accepting your 2 free books and 2 free gifts (gifts valued at approximately $10.00) places you under no obligation to buy anything. You may keep the books and gifts and return the shipping statement marked "cancel." If you do not cancel, about a month later we'll send you 6 additional books and bill you just $4.55 each in the U.S. or $4.99 each in Canada. That is a savings of at least 13% off the cover price. It's quite a bargain! Shipping and handling is just 50¢ per book in the U.S. and 75¢ per book in Canada.* You may cancel at any time, but if you choose to continue, every month we'll send you 6 more books, which you may either purchase at the discount price or return to us and cancel your subscription.

*Terms and prices subject to change without notice. Prices do not include applicable taxes. Sales tax applicable in N.Y. Canadian residents will be charged applicable taxes. Offer not valid in Quebec. Books received may not be as shown. All orders subject to credit approval. Credit or debit balances in a customer's account(s) may be offset by any other outstanding balance owed by or to the customer. Please allow 4 to 6 weeks for delivery. Offer available while quantities last.

here to see Channing." And without waiting to be invited inside, he moved past the man before turning back to him. "Where is she?"

The man looked at him curiously, as if to size him up. Then he said, "She's in the kitchen."

"Not anymore," Channing said, frowning as she stepped into the living room carrying an armful of food containers. She had heard Zane's voice and could not believe his audacity. Why was he still in Virginia? More importantly, why was he here?

"Let me help you with those," Ronald said, quickly moving forward to relieve her of the stack she was carrying.

"Thanks."

She glanced over at Zane and saw the deep haze of anger in his eyes. What was his problem? Deciding to wait until Ronald left before confronting Zane as to why he was here, she said, "Ronald, I'd like you to meet Zane. An old friend."

Juggling the containers in one hand, Ronald moved toward Zane with the other hand outstretched. "Nice meeting you."

Zane accepted the man's handshake grudgingly. "You stay around these parts, Ronald?" Zane asked.

Channing frowned. "Yes, Ronald stays next door," she answered for him. "His wife and kids are here for the summer."

"Wife?" Zane asked, shifting his gaze from Ronald to Channing.

"Yes, *wife*," Channing answered, annoyed.

She then smiled at Ronald. "I hope you, Jennifer and the kids enjoy everything."

Ronald returned her smile. "I'm sure we will, and

again we appreciate it." Then with a concerned look on his face, he asked Channing, "You're going to be okay?"

Channing knew why he was asking. Evidently he'd picked up on Zane's anger and figured Zane might be an old friend but, at the moment, a bad-tempered one. "Yes, I'll be fine."

Satisfied with her response, Ronald glanced back at Zane. "Nice meeting you, Zane."

"Yeah, same here." Zane quickly moved to open the door for the man. When the door closed behind Ronald, he turned to Channing. Ignoring the scowl on her face, a smile curved his lips. "He seems like a nice married guy."

Her frown indicated that she had not appreciated his initial churlish attitude toward Ronald. "What are you doing here, Zane? I thought you'd be back in Denver by now," she said, turning.

He followed her into the kitchen.

"Not sure why you thought that. Besides, I've been doing a lot of thinking about our conver—"

He stopped talking as he looked around, seeing her kitchen table and counter littered with food containers. "What's going on? You're opening a restaurant on the side?"

Channing rolled her eyes when she began placing some of the containers in the refrigerator. "No, I was just in the mood to cook yesterday."

"All of this?"

She frowned over her shoulder. "Yes, all of this. I decided to share some with Ronald and Jennifer. They have a sweet little girl and a son who hasn't started walking yet. They're a beautiful family."

He nodded, thinking those folks were not as beautiful as his and Channing's family would be one day.

Last night, after he'd planned his strategy, he'd envisioned them married with a couple of kids and living happily at the Hideout.

"So why did you come back, Zane?"

He leaned against the counter. "I couldn't help myself."

Channing drew in a deep sigh. She hoped he wasn't back to confusing lust with love again. "What do you mean you couldn't help yourself?" she asked, lifting one eyebrow.

He shoved his hands into the pockets of his jeans. "I got to thinking about our conversation yesterday."

"And?"

"I told you I loved you, but you didn't believe me. You said I'm confusing lust with love. For the sake of argument, let's say you're right about that."

"I am right," she said with absolute certainty. "No man, or woman for that matter, who's been against falling in love to the depth that you have can miraculously wake up one morning and decide they're in love. Falling in love doesn't work that way."

Zane nodded. "Okay, let's say you're right."

"And?"

Now to throw out the hook and hope she takes the bait, Zane thought as he moved closer. "And if it's only lust, like you claim, because of this strong sexual chemistry between us, then the only thing I have to say is that I feel that I'm close."

She lifted a brow. "Close to what?"

"Falling in love with you."

Channing closed the refrigerator, thinking that now she'd heard everything. "Falling in love with me?"

"Yes. Close. According to you, I can't be in love with you. If you're right about that, then how come when that guy opened the door I was ready to hurt him when I thought—"

"I know what you thought, Zane," Channing interrupted him to say. "And even if that was the case, it wasn't any of your business."

He straightened, rolling his head around and working his shoulders to slog out the kinks. "It might not be my business, but it's an example of one of those things that I can't help where you're concerned. I've never gotten jealous over a woman before, Channing, so that has to mean something."

She met his gaze. "It does mean something, and it has nothing to do with love. It means you're possessive. You don't want me, but you don't want anyone else to have me, either."

"You make me sound like a selfish bastard."

"Well…it's a description that fits," she said, moving around him to go into the living room. In fact, she was leading him to the door. She thought of a question she'd meant to ask him yesterday—something that had nagged at her all during the night. She turned, and he almost bumped into her. When he reached out his hand to steady her, her body tingled from the contact. She forced herself to take a step back when he dropped his hand.

"I have a question for you," she said, trying to downplay the sensations that were still moving through her body.

"What?"

Channing caught her lower lip between her teeth as she thought about what she wanted to ask him. She decided to come out and do it. "Would it have made a difference if you hadn't thought Mack was cheating on me?"

"What do you mean?" he asked, leaning against a wall in her living room.

"If you hadn't assumed Mack was cheating on me, would you have seduced me, anyway?"

He didn't hesitate. "Yes."

She stiffened. "Why?"

It seemed as if several long seconds ticked between them before he responded. "I wanted you, and I could tell you wanted me. I know your body, Channing. I knew the moment you became wet for me. The moment your nipples hardened. I didn't have to wait for you to ask to know you wanted me inside of you."

Channing's stomach clenched. That wetness he was talking about, heaven help her. His words had it flowing again. She felt disgusted with herself for letting Zane have this kind of power over her.

Deciding she needed to take a stand against what he'd claimed regardless of whether it had merit or not, she said, "So you decided to act on your assumption? Even while believing I was engaged to marry another man? The Zane Westmoreland I know would not have done that."

He moved, coming within inches of her. "Then maybe I'm not the Zane you thought you knew."

Evidently not.

During those months they'd dated, she had been sure of him regardless of what he'd said about love. But he'd proved her wrong, which was why she couldn't believe his claim of love. Now it seemed she'd been right not to believe him. He was only on the verge of love.

"I think you should leave now," she said, moving again toward the door. When she opened it, he reached around her and shut it. She saw a muscle working in his jaw.

"What do you think you're doing?" she asked.

"I came back today for a reason, Channing."

She narrowed her gaze at him. "I know, you couldn't help yourself because now you think there's a chance that you're falling in love with me." Channing shook her head. "Deliberate or otherwise, you're confusing the heck out of me. Maybe you're right, and you aren't the Zane I thought I knew. If that's true, I don't want to know the Zane that you are now."

She gasped when he braced strong arms against the door on either side of her, effectively trapping her. "Maybe you should."

Zane knew what he'd told her was true. He wasn't the same Zane. First of all, the old Zane would never have fallen in love, and he loved this woman so much he ached all over.

"You're not making much sense, Zane."

He almost agreed with her, but he knew what he was doing *did* make sense. It was his strategy to win her over, to prove once and for all that what he felt for her wasn't lust but love. "Two years ago you thought you knew me, Channing. I enjoyed you, and you enjoyed me. In your neat and tidy world, you figured things should move from point A to point B by nobody's timetable but your own. However, what you failed to figure into the equation is that the worst thing a woman can do is push a man when he isn't ready. You did that. I wasn't ready then. I am now."

He saw irritation spread across her face. "Ready for what?"

"To be pushed into feeling things I wasn't ready to feel before. In fact, I'm open to endless possibilities."

Channing stared at Zane as her mind trickled back in

time. The Zane Westmoreland she'd fallen in love with had never been a typical guy. There had been so many facets to him that she'd spent the first couple of months of their relationship trying to unravel him. There had been the reserved Zane. The forbidding Zane. The Zane who was devoted to his family. The Zane who said what he meant and meant what he said. Those were the qualities that had first attracted her to him, and those same qualities were what had captured her heart and made her fall in love with him.

She knew he still had those qualities, so who was the Zane she didn't know? As if the question was stamped on her forehead for him to read, he said, "You never get to know anyone completely, Channing, and the reason I'm willing to be pushed now is because I don't want to lose you again." He paused. "I admit I'm close. Closer than I've ever been in my entire life. Like I said, all I need is a little push."

He had to make Channing understand. He loved her, and maybe if she didn't believe he was there already, she would buy that he was almost there and take the chance of prodding him further.

"I admire you so damn much, Channing," he said honestly. "More than any other woman I've been involved with. I knew you wanted more from me, more than I could give. But that didn't mean I didn't care for you, because I did. I never led you on. I was always honest with you."

Channing said nothing as she thought about what he said. He was right. He had always been honest with her. He'd never told her he loved her, and she could admit that it wasn't his fault that she had wanted him to feel differently.

Now he needs a little push. What if I give him that

*push and nothing comes of it? Doesn't he understand
he's asking me to play Russian roulette with my heart?*

"Just what are you asking of me, Zane?"

"Something I probably have no right to," he said
gently. "But I'm asking anyway because I want you
more than I've ever wanted any woman. Don't give up
on me. Get to know the real Zane, and don't be afraid to
push me to the limit. You're the only woman who can.
You're the only woman I will ever love."

Channing drew in a deep breath as she absorbed
what Zane was saying. Although he didn't love her, he
believed that she had the power to make him love her?
All he needed was a little push. If that was the case, why
hadn't he fallen in love with her when they were dating? Things had been good between them—the sex, the
communication, the entire relationship. He hadn't been
ready then. What would be different this time around?

She drew in another deep breath, deciding to call
him out on something he'd said yesterday. "When you
said you loved me, one of the reasons you claimed you
didn't act on it was because you were afraid. What did
you mean by that?"

Zane held her gaze for a long time, then in a quiet
tone he said, "Let's sit down while I try to explain
things."

She stared at him a second before nodding. What he
was about to tell her was the complete truth. He hoped
it would help her understand him. When she led him
into the living room, he followed. She eased down on
the sofa, and he took the chair across from her.

Channing sensed by the firm set of his chin that
whatever Zane was about to tell her was a serious matter. He was sitting in the chair, stiff and straight, which
indicated that he was not comfortable with what he was

about to share. Gone were his familiar coolness, relaxed air and arrogance. Instead, she detected a sense of vulnerability in him—one that was controlled and guarded. Those were things she hadn't seen in him before.

He was tense, and she could feel the tension, as well. Why? "Zane?"

He met her gaze, held it for a long moment and then he asked softly, "Can you imagine losing both your parents at the same time?"

Channing's pulse almost stopped. She swallowed deeply as she truthfully answered his question. "No, I can't."

He nodded slowly. "Well, I did. I was only nineteen and in my second year of college when it happened. But not only did I lose my parents. I also lost my uncle and aunt, who were like parents to me, as well. From that day forward, my life hasn't been the same."

Channing didn't say anything. Because of her friendship with Megan, she knew the story of how his parents and his aunt and uncle had lost their lives in a plane crash. She'd also known there had been several Westmoreland kids under the age of sixteen at the time and that Zane's brother Ramsey and his cousin Dillon had worked hard and made sacrifices to keep the family together.

"There wasn't a whole lot of time for grieving since we had to all pitch in to help the younger ones cope. It wasn't easy. A few of them worked through their grief by being rebellious, which caused unnecessary drama for all of us. But the one thing I decided never to do, because of that experience, was to get attached to anyone who I could lose in that way."

After a deep breath, he continued. "I loved my parents, and losing them was hard on me. The pain was deep—almost unbearable at times. Unless you've been through something like that, you can't begin to understand."

Channing believed it. She could hear the pain in his voice and could also see it in his eyes. "Is that the reason you can't fall in love, Zane? For fear of losing that person?"

"I thought so, but when I thought I had lost you after that night in McKays, for the first time I felt like I could take the risk. The risk of loving you was greater than the fear."

So he thought he could be pushed into falling in love with her, she surmised, because she was the first woman he had felt so strongly connected to that the positive emotions overrode his ingrained fear. Was his admission enough for them to move forward and try again?

Could she actually push him into loving her?

What he was asking went against everything she'd ever read in relationship books. A woman couldn't seduce a man into loving her. It took both people to make a relationship work. Was she missing some point here? Had she failed to take into account that all relationships weren't the same? Had she been so focused on what she'd wanted out of the relationship that she'd refused to see that he couldn't be rushed?

Zane had been a psychology major while in college and was rumored to have the ability to get into a woman's psyche and fully understand how females perceived their world. If that was the case, maybe it was high time for a woman to determine how he perceived his.

For nine months, they'd shared a traditional relationship. They had met, shared great chemistry, enjoyed mind-blowing sex, found it easy to communicate with each other and had a good friendship. No game-playing and no pressure. Yet in the end, love hadn't blossomed... at least not on his end.

But what if he doesn't fall head over heels in love with you? Well, if that happens, at least you'll have no doubt in your mind that he has issues that can't be solved. There is a slim chance that what he says is true, that he's capable of falling in love with you.

Are you willing to do whatever is necessary to find out? Even if it means putting on those rose-colored glasses and unlocking your heart again?

He stared at her with his mesmerizing eyes. Heat pooled between her legs because of his intense focus. The idea that he was asking her to help him fall in love was too much to take in at the moment. But if he hadn't fallen in love before because he'd been afraid to love, could she help erase his fears?

"Go out with me tonight, Channing," he said, his words floating across the room and touching her skin like a caress. "I understand there's one of those drive-in theaters around here."

When she parted her lips to turn him down, he held up his hand. "Before you say no, just think about what fun it might be. I haven't been to one in years. I remember my folks would pile us all into their car, and it was great. And guess what? It's John Travolta Night. *Saturday Night Fever* and *Grease* are in the lineup. I know how much you like the guy."

He was right. She was a big John Travolta fan. There wasn't a movie he'd made that she hadn't seen. "John Travolta Night?"

"Yes."

She knew that accepting his invitation to the movies meant she was accepting his challenge. Was that something she wanted? Should she turn him down and ask him to leave and not come back?

No, she couldn't do that. Doing so would be giving up on him, and if there was a possibility—even a slim one—that he was on the verge of falling in love with her, then she wanted to see it through. Who was it who said if you wanted something badly enough it was worth fighting for?

But this time if she wanted to do things differently, she had to shake up their routine.

"Yes, I'll go to the drive-in theater with you, but you can get rid of the condoms. I won't be having sex with you."

"You won't?"

"No."

Zane didn't say anything while he thought about her request. Evidently she was still trying to understand this lust-versus-love thing. That was fine, because he would show her that his love encompassed everything—both the physical and the emotional. Besides, they wouldn't be having sex because they'd never had sex in the first place. They'd always made love, and it seemed he needed to show her the difference.

"Okay, Channing, we won't have sex."

As soon as he said the words, he saw what seemed to be anxiety leave her gaze. She stood. "I'll walk you to the door now."

He stood, too, and followed her. When they reached the door, they faced each other. Zane stroked Channing's hair while her gaze locked with his. How could he not have known the depth of his love for her before now? Why had it taken losing her a second time to make him realize that he could not handle losing her again?

"I'll be back around six." Deciding to give her something to look forward to, he leaned toward her, placed his hands at her waist and said in a soft, husky tone, "Go ahead and try it now, Channing. Push."

"I don't think—"

"Push," he encouraged again.

He heard her soft sigh and then a whisper when she said his name. "Zane."

When she boldly licked the tip of her tongue across his lips his breath caught and heat settled in his groin. He inhaled deeply and discovered her scent was as erotic and sensual as ever. Channing's unique aroma had the ability to drive him crazy... It was doing so now.

"You want to be pushed," she whispered across his moist lips. "Then you're going to get just what you ask for. When I finish with you, your heart won't be the same, Zane."

He had news for her. It was already different, and he would take great pleasure in proving it to her. When she took a step back and reached out to open the door, he reminded her, "I'll be back around six."

"Okay."

He walked out of her door knowing any moves he made on her would be the most important ones of his life.

His campaign would begin tonight. Already his mind buzzed with ideas for ways he could make the evening unforgettable.

Nine

Channing picked up her cell phone when she saw the caller was Megan. "Hey, Megan, what's up?"

"Thought I'd ask you the same thing. Rico confessed that he told Zane where you were. Sorry about that."

Channing eased down on the sofa. "No reason to apologize and yes, Zane showed up on my doorstep yesterday."

"And?"

"And he claimed he loved me."

There was an undisputed gasp. "Zane told you that?"

"Yes. But of course I don't believe him."

"You don't?"

"No. It was less than a week ago when he looked me right in the eyes and told me he *didn't* love me, that what he felt for me was nothing more than possession. In other words, Zane thinks I'm his and doesn't want me to belong to another man. Now he wants me to believe he woke up one morning and miraculously realized he loves me. That's hogwash, and you know it."

"And you told him you didn't believe him?"

"Yes, and I asked that he leave." Channing decided there was no reason to mention she'd had sex with him before he left.

"So now he's on his way back to Denver?"

There was a pause before Channing said, "Not exactly. He showed up here again this morning."

"And?"

"And he did a flip-flop on me."

"Flip-flop? Now he's saying that he doesn't love you?"

Channing heard confusion in Megan's voice, so she tried to explain. "He's admitting to feeling things for me he hasn't felt for any other woman. I guess those emotions are confusing him, and he believes that if what he's feeling isn't love yet then it's close to it. He says all he needs is a little push."

"A little push by whom?"

"Me."

Megan frowned. She'd never heard anything so ridiculous in her life.

But the more she thought about it, the more she could see Zane's ploy even if Channing couldn't. First of all, there was no doubt in her mind that Zane loved Channing. He would not have dropped everything to go after her if he didn't. Then there was his admission of love. Zane would never admit loving someone if he actually didn't. And as far as him miraculously waking up one morning and realizing how he felt about Channing—well Channing might not believe it could happen that way, but Megan did.

Channing was dealing with a Westmoreland male,

and most Denver Westmoreland males had put up road-blocks when it came to falling in love. Ramsey, Derringer and Riley had fought the idea of falling in love tooth and nail. Even she and her sister Gemma hadn't given up their hearts easily.

Knowing how that analytical and psychological mind of Zane's tended to work, Megan knew his plan. He figured that since Channing didn't believe him, he would show her the evolution. He'd even gone so far as to encourage Channing to spearhead the transformation. Megan hated to admit it, but it was a brilliant strategy—if it worked. And she had a feeling it *would* work because Zane never failed at anything that he put his mind to. And he had an additional advantage. His heart was in it, as well.

"So, are you going to do it?" Megan heard herself asking.

There was a moment of silence and then Channing said, "Yes. I love him so much, Megan, even though I don't want to. Zane is a complex man." She paused then added, "He explained how your parents' and uncle's and aunt's deaths affected him."

Megan's mouth dropped open. "He told you that?" She was stunned that Zane would be that forthcoming about his fears. Over the years, she'd suspected he felt that way but had never been sure.

"Yes, he told me. And if that's really the reason he's been holding back then maybe I can help him overcome that. Do you think I'm crazy for thinking that way?"

Megan drew in a deep breath and smiled. "I see nothing wrong with a woman fighting for the love of her man, Channing." Just like she saw nothing wrong with a man fighting for the love of his woman. Crazy thing was, Zane and Channing were fighting for the same thing, and neither of them knew it yet.

"I'm going to keep my fingers crossed that things work out for you," Megan said quietly.

"Thanks, Megan. I appreciate it."

The rest of the day moved pretty fast for Zane. So he didn't feel like a slacker while he was in Virginia Beach and Jason and Derringer were back in Denver hard at work, the three of them had agreed that Zane could sort through the online files that had been piling up for months. Using his tablet computer, he had gone through all the emails, trashing a lot of spam and making appointments for interested horse buyers.

Now he glanced at the clock. He had a couple of hours before he picked up Channing, and he had a number of things to do. The hotel would be preparing a basket of food and wine. And when he had stopped at one of the gift shops downstairs he'd seen the perfect wine glasses and told the hotel he wanted them included in the basket, as well. When he was younger, his parents would take him and his siblings to Denver's only drive-in theater. It had closed ages ago, but those times had definitely been fun for them. Bailey had been in diapers and the twins were barely saying words that you could understand. Too bad Zane hadn't known that memories such as those were ones he would have to cherish forever.

As he slid into his jacket, he realized he wanted to share that special drive-in magic with Channing. He knew she wasn't keen on going to the movies with him—or to a drive-in theater of all places. But he thought that was just the kind of place they needed. At the drive-in, they wouldn't have to worry about anyone sitting beside them, invading their space. They would be in the car all alone.

He shook his head at his predicament. He figured after a week or so Channing would realize he loved her. If not, then he intended to sit down and try again to give it to her straight. Regardless of what she believed, he was a man who knew his mind and his heart.

Zane smiled as he headed for the door. She should have gotten the flowers by now. It wasn't the first time he'd sent a woman flowers, but it was the first time sending them had ever really meant anything to him.

"Ma'am? Will you be signing for the flowers?"

Channing blinked, but she still saw the man standing on her porch holding not just a vase of flowers but what looked like an entire friggin' bush. And they were roses. Red ones. The most beautiful flowers she'd ever seen. "Oh, yes," she said, coming to her senses. She quickly scribbled her name on the pad he'd given her.

"Where do you want me to place these? I doubt you can carry them."

She doubted it, as well. "This way," she said, leading the middle-aged man into her living room. "Right here will do."

She stared as he set the potted bush down and stepped back. "Whoever sent these probably meant for you to plant this outside. I've never seen anything so large. He didn't just send you long-stemmed roses. He sent you the entire rosebush."

Channing nodded. "Wait a second so I can give you a tip."

"No need," he said, heading toward the door. "It's already been taken care of. Your guy thought of everything. Nice fellow."

Yeah, nice fellow, she thought, closing the door behind the deliveryman and turning to stare at the bush again. She'd read the card already and knew exactly who'd sent them, and she couldn't forget what the card had said.

I love you.

What in the world was going on in that head of Zane's? Why was he trying to get a head start on falling in love when she hadn't even started pushing him yet?

She glanced over at the clock and then hurried to her bedroom. He would be here in less than thirty minutes, and she still had to put on her makeup. Good thing she never used a whole lot. Just a little powder and lipstick. Zane had often complimented her on her natural beauty.

She was wearing a pair of shorts and a tank top; she figured she'd keep them on. After all, she and Zane were going to a drive-in. If they decided to grab something to eat later, they could go to a fast-food place. Or they could come back here since she had plenty of food in the refrigerator.

She tossed her hair back from her face and tossed the idea from her head. She didn't need to give Zane any encouragement by inviting him to her house after the movies. She would push, but it would be on her time and in her own way.

She drew in a deep breath when she heard his knock. Giving herself one last check in the full-length mirror, she left her bedroom and headed for the door.

When Channing opened the door, Zane shoved his hands into the pockets of his slacks and looked down at himself. He then glanced up at her and smiled. "I think I might be a little overdressed."

A smile touched Channing's lips when she stepped

aside to let him in. "Yes, I would say just a little. We're just going to the drive-in, Zane. No need for the jacket, shirt and slacks. You could have worn shorts or jeans with a T-shirt."

He shrugged. "I don't own a pair of shorts."

She lifted a brow. "You're kidding."

He chuckled. "No, why would I kid about something like that? Have you forgotten I live in Colorado?"

"No, but there are warm days there. In fact, I remember a few times during the summer when it got up in the nineties."

"Possibly, but I feel more comfortable in jeans or long pants. If there's a problem with what I'm wearing, I can go back by the hotel and change."

She waved off his words. "No problem. I'm fine with it. I just want you to be comfortable."

"Oh, I plan to be comfortable."

"Okay, then. Are you ready? All I have to do is—"

"Come here," he interrupted in a low, husky tone, pulling her into his arms. "You look good, and you smell good, too."

She went to him easily, willingly. Doing so reminded her of the time when things had been so good for them. A time when she had felt sure of herself where he was concerned. "Thank you. And I should also be thanking you for the flowers. Or should I say the rosebush. It's beautiful."

"So are you."

"Thank you. Now as far as the card is concerned…"

"What about it?" He continued holding her in his arms. It was as though this was where she was meant to be.

"Getting carried away, don't you think? Not giving me much room to push."

He feigned ignorance. "You think so?"

"Yes."

"You think I'm moving too fast?"

Channing sighed deeply before pulling herself from his embrace and taking a step back. He could see the irritation in her expression. "What you're doing is saying things you don't mean. So chill, okay?"

He did mean them, and he intended for her to know it. But for now… "Okay. Are you ready to go?"

"Yes, let me grab my tote bag."

As she rushed toward her bedroom, he noticed the huge plant sitting in the corner. When he'd walked into the florist shop after leaving her house earlier today, he'd seen it and wanted her to have it. He knew from the months they'd been together that she liked roses, especially red ones. Yet he'd never sent her any. On those occasions when he had sent her flowers, she'd gotten the pink-and-white carnations like all the other women he'd dated. He had been intent on not changing his course. The last thing he'd wanted was to fill her mind with the hope that things were more serious between them than they actually were. In a way, this rosebush represented all the roses he should have given her and hadn't.

"I'm ready."

He smiled at her. "Okay, then. Let's go."

Taking hold of her arm, he led her toward the door.

"It seems you thought of everything," Channing said, noting the large basket in the backseat. She wasn't sure what was in it, but she was impressed he'd brought it.

"I tried to. We can eat whenever you get hungry."

She had eaten a nice lunch right after Megan's call, and it had filled her up. But that was before she'd gotten into Zane's rental car and the basket had snagged her attention.

To get her mind and her stomach off the basket, she examined her surroundings. She saw all the cars parked facing the huge screen. A little excitement ran through her body. This was something new for her. "This is nice," she said. "And this is the first time I've been to a drive-in."

Zane let his seat back to accommodate his long legs. He glanced over at Channing. "You've never been to one before?"

"No. How old do you think I am? I understand drive-in theaters are nearly as extinct as dinosaurs."

"They aren't *that* extinct," he said, chuckling. "I used to go to one every Saturday night with my parents. They would load all of us into the van. It was fun. The one we went to even had a playground."

"Wow, you remember all of that?"

He nodded. "Yes. Those were special times for us, especially for me. After the folks died, that's all I had left. The memories. My counselor suggested I write it down."

She arched a brow. "Counselor?"

"Yes. Mrs. Harris. She was a grief counselor. Dillon and Ramsey thought it would be a good idea if we all went to see her. I think that's when I decided I wanted to become a psychologist."

She followed his lead and pressed the lever to let her seat back. Her legs weren't as long as his, but it felt nice to stretch out. "You have a degree in psychology, yet you've never used it in your work. Why?"

"Because by the time I finished college it was all hands on deck at Blue Ridge Land Management," he said. Blue Ridge was the family firm that his father and uncle had left behind. "Dillon and Ramsey were doing all they could to keep things going, and I felt my rightful place was to be there to help them. It was all about sacrifices."

He shifted in his seat to face her. "In a way, going to work for Blue Ridge was a blessing."

"In what way?"

"It showed me that I'm not suited for being indoors behind a desk. After a while, I felt boxed in. Caged. I knew that I couldn't be a psychologist. I needed to work outside."

"Then that partnership with your cousins came at the right time."

He smiled. "Yes. Mainly because Derringer and Jason were ready to bail from Blue Ridge, as well. The three of us love horses, and our fathers taught us to ride when we were knee-high. So when our cousins in Montana decided to expand their horse training and breeding business, there was no doubt in our minds that we were on board."

She nodded. One of the things she'd missed after leaving Denver was talking to Zane. They had a rapport that had made it easy to talk about anything. Or almost anything. She'd just realized he had never before shared with her why he'd pursued a degree in psychology instead of a degree in business like his brother Derringer and several of his cousins. She knew his brother Ramsey had gone to school for some type of agricultural degree since he'd always wanted to be a sheep rancher.

"Was Dillon upset because the three of you defected at once?"

Zane chuckled. "No, he understood. He'd known Blue Ridge wasn't in our blood any more than it had been in Ramsey's. Some people are born to be corporate leaders, and some are not. Besides, Riley and Stern were eager to take their places at the company. Even Canyon was gung ho once he decided being a doctor wasn't for him."

The huge screen flared to life. When it showed visuals of what they had for sale at the snack bar, Channing heard her stomach growl. She glanced over at Zane. "Sorry."

"No need to apologize. If you're hungry, just grab something out of that basket. I have a lot of good stuff in there. Better stuff than what you're seeing on the screen."

Of course after he'd said that, Channing had to check it out and make sure. Taking off her seat belt, she rose up in the seat on her knees and reached in the backseat to uncover the basket. She was impressed. There were several meaty-looking sub sandwiches, bags of chips, an assortment of fruit and a bottle of red wine. Her favorite. But what really caught her eye were the two wine glasses. They were engraved in a beautiful gold script. One had her name on it, and the other had his.

A deep stirring spread in the center of Channing's stomach. Why would he go out and do something like that? She grabbed a couple of sandwiches, the bottle of wine and both glasses. Turning back around, she straightened in her seat but didn't put the seat belt back on.

She held up her bounty. "Nice wine glasses."

"Thanks. I happened to see them in the hotel's gift shop. I thought, wow, imagine that. Our names."

Channing threw her head back and laughed. He was lying through his teeth. "Come on. Names like Channing and Zane? You want me to believe there's another…" She stopped, coming short of saying the word *couple*. They were no longer a couple.

Zane didn't have any misgivings. He finished the sentence for her. "Couple like us? Probably not, since we're unique."

She shrugged and handed him a sandwich. He took it, and she opened the wine and poured them both glasses. She handed his to him and said, "Um, smell the aroma. Isn't it wonderful?"

He took a sip, met her gaze and held it. "I like your aroma better."

Channing swallowed, wishing he hadn't said that. It was bad enough sharing such close quarters with him, but to have him draw any level of intimacy into their conversation was too much. To keep things safe, she decided not to respond to what he'd said.

He'd told her often how he loved her scent, how it would turn him on. Well, she hoped he remembered their agreement about no sex. She wasn't so sure he *did* remember—the car's windows were tinted where no one could see them. Channing couldn't help wondering if that was by choice or coincidence.

Before she could dwell on it any longer, the screen blared the announcement that the first movie was about to begin. So she ate her sandwich and sipped her wine while silence reigned between them. She refused to glance over at him. Instead, she stared straight ahead at the huge movie screen.

Zane's blood pressure had spiked. He took a sip of his wine while eating his sandwich. Reaching back into the basket for a bag of chips, he ate them, as well. He enjoyed the meal all while inhaling Channing's scent.

How had he gone two years without the aroma he'd become addicted to?

He knew women pretty damn well. Every woman had her own unique scent. He knew the power that pheromones could have on a man. Channing had a way of luring him in with her scent each and every time.

Trying to get his mind off Channing for the time being, he wondered if the drive-in theaters would become a fad again. Gone were the days when you had to park next to a speaker pole and pull the speaker in through your car's window. Due to modern technology, the sound was now transmitted through your car's radio. Nice.

Because they'd arrived early, the lines had not been long, and they had found a good parking spot. The view of the screen was spectacular. He wasn't a big John Travolta fan, but he knew Channing was. When he'd inquired at the hotel about where to take his lady that was casual, different and fun, the concierge had mentioned this place. Zane was glad he had.

Finally, he couldn't help himself. He glanced over at Channing, only to find that it seemed as though she was really absorbed in the movie. How many times had she seen *Grease?* He'd given her the DVD, and when it had come to Denver as a play, he'd taken her to see that, as well.

She had finished off her sandwich and the last of her wine. "Want more wine?"

She gazed over at him. "No, I've had enough. Thanks."

She turned back to the movie, but he continued watching her. Damn, he loved her. Whether she believed him or not, it had happened just the way he'd told her. The realization might have been late in coming, but it had punched him hard, first in the heart and then right between the eyes, making him see things he hadn't seen before.

If she needed to see his transformation to believe him, then a transformation was what she would get. Tonight, he was starting off slow, smooth and seductive. He reached across the seat and took her hand in his. They used to hold hands all the time, but he could tell she was somewhat surprised by his gesture. She didn't pull her hand away, but it felt stiff in his.

"Relax, Channing. I just want to hold your hand."

"Why?"

He could say he wanted to do it because he loved her and he enjoyed touching her, but he figured she wasn't ready to buy that. "I just do, okay?"

She shrugged with tense shoulders. "Okay."

"And before you get rigid and unbending, I haven't forgotten your 'no sex' rule."

She relaxed somewhat. "I was beginning to wonder."

He chuckled. "Why?"

"Because you're touching me."

He lifted a brow. "Was I not supposed to?"

She shook her head. "It brings back memories."

He smiled. "But memories are good, right?"

Her chin lifted. "Some are. Some aren't."

The last thing he wanted was for her to think about the bad memories he'd caused. "Slide over here for a minute," he said, tightening his hand on hers.

She hesitated but then slid across the seat toward him. He folded up the center console to make a bench seat. He didn't want anything separating them. Satisfied with their closeness, he wrapped his arms around her shoulders. "That's better. I like you plastered against me like this. I missed this, Channing. The closeness.

The intimacy," he said truthfully. He hadn't realized just how much until now.

"It was your choice," she said, and he heard the bitterness in her tone.

"I know. My mistake," he countered softly.

She glanced over at him, and he saw the reservation in her eyes. He knew he would do anything to remove that look. "It was hard for me after you left, Channing."

"Was it?"

She asked as if she didn't believe him. "Yes. I was in a bad way mainly because I couldn't believe you'd left. You said you were leaving. You even went through all the motions of leaving, but I just couldn't get it through my head that you were actually going to do it. For a long time, I was in a state of denial."

She frowned, narrowing her eyes. "Why? Because you're the great Zane Westmoreland, and women aren't supposed to leave you? It's supposed to be the other way around?"

He didn't say anything for a minute. "I thought that was the reason at first," he said truthfully. "But then…"

She looked searchingly at him. "But what?"

"I felt the loss," he said hoarsely. "I actually felt it. And when it hit me that you wouldn't be back, I developed a bad attitude. It was so awful that no one in my family wanted to be around me. Dillon had to step in a few times to keep me and my other cousins or brothers from exchanging blows. I was filled with so much anger that just about anything could set me off."

Channing stayed silent. She'd talked to Megan a few times after moving to Atlanta, and his sister hadn't mentioned anything about Zane's bad temperament. But then she and Megan had agreed not to bring him up in any of their conversations. However, hearing what he was saying now made her ask, "Why, Zane? Why did my leaving upset you when you told me there could never be anything permanent between us?"

Zane sighed deeply as he thought about what she'd asked. How could he link the fear he'd felt at her departure to the same fear he'd felt when his parents had died? After she'd left Denver, he hadn't been able to handle the loneliness and emptiness within him. And when he had compared those feelings to the void he hadn't ever wanted to feel again, he'd withdrawn. He'd resolved never to let down his guard with any woman like he'd done with her.

"Zane?"

He could hear impatience in her voice. She wanted an answer, and he knew she deserved one. However, how could he explain it in a way that she would understand? A way where she could connect the dots the way he finally had?

Zane held her gaze and forced himself not to pull her into his arms and kiss her instead of answering her. He couldn't do that this time. He had to make sure he laid out everything she needed to see.

"You left me, Channing. At first, I convinced myself that it didn't matter, that you were doing the right thing because I couldn't give you what you wanted. But then…"

She leaned toward him. "Yes?"

He spoke truthfully when he said, "Then I began to feel like a piece of me was gone. I felt empty. My emptiness turned to anger because I had sworn I would never let myself feel such pain over a loss again."

An uneasy feeling raced up Channing's spine as she stared at Zane, the movie forgotten. Hearing him say those words had an insurmountable effect on her. Had that been when he'd realized he might feel something for her?

If what he said was true, then she could see why he'd gotten upset when she'd returned almost two years later with a fiancé. But it didn't explain or excuse his behavior at McKays. She had given him a chance to tell her he loved her, but he hadn't. Instead, he'd seduced her to prove a point.

"I had to leave," she said softly. "I could not stay in Denver and pretend I was okay in a relationship that wasn't going anywhere." She released a deep sigh. "Maybe this whole 'pushing' thing isn't a good idea, Zane."

"What makes you say that?"

"If it doesn't work, I'm the only one who'll get hurt. After McKays, I left Denver in pain for the second time with no plans to ever return or to ever see you again. Then, low and behold, you show up yesterday and the next thing you know we're having sex for old time's sake. You came back again today and convinced me that all it will take is a little push to get you to fall in love. But if I couldn't do it during the nine months we were together, what difference will it make now?"

He heard the doubt in her voice. The frustration. He wouldn't be happy until he heard certainty. Absolute and complete. When all was said and done, he wanted her misgivings to be put behind them…mainly because he wanted her to know she had his heart.

She pulled back and looked at him with a narrowed gaze. "Is this nothing but a game to you, Zane? A game to see how far you can make me go without giving me a commitment? Or maybe it's revenge. You're getting back at me for having the nerve to leave you in the first place. You like proving points."

He leaned forward. "Although I know it's hard for you, I'm asking you to trust me. I wouldn't be here if I didn't care about you, Channing." He ran his fingers through her hair. "You mean everything to me."

Channing drew in a deep breath. Zane knew exactly what he was doing. She'd always loved the feel of his hands in her hair. There was something about the way he did it that sent tingling sensations through her.

The silence between them lengthened. She closed her eyes, wishing she could pretend those two years without him had never happened and things were as they used to be. Maybe if she and Zane had stayed together, if she hadn't tried to rush things along, they might be married by now. That possibility was why she was here now. Taking another chance on him.

"What are you thinking about?" he asked her in a low voice.

She opened her eyes and looked at him. His face was right there, inches from hers. "It doesn't matter."

"Everything about this matters, Channing."

She wished she could believe that.

"Ask me what I'm thinking," he said throatily.

They should be watching the movie. Wasn't that what they'd come here for? she asked herself.

No. The reason they were here together was to see if they could repair their damaged relationship. To see if he could love her the way she needed to be loved. To see if he could really love her the way he thought he could. "Okay. What are you thinking, Zane?"

"How beautiful you are for starters."

His hand left her hair and moved to her chin. He tilted her face up to his. "Very beautiful."

"You can't see very well," she whispered. His lips were close to hers. She knew those lips well. Full and inviting, they had the ability to make liquid heat fill her. Just thinking about how well she knew those lips, her firsthand knowledge of how they tasted, had her feminine muscles clenching.

"I can see just fine, Channing. And you know what else I was thinking about?"

She swallowed tightly, knowing it was best not to respond but unable to hold back. "No, what?"

"This." And then he leaned in, capturing her lips with his.

Ten

Zane knew that Channing couldn't deny that kissing was one means of communication they both enjoyed. And he wasn't about to make it a quick kiss. On the contrary. He intended to play it out for as long as he could and redefine in her mind just what a Zane Westmoreland kiss was all about. He was fighting to keep control, but the mating of their tongues made it difficult. Nearly impossible. He felt weak in the knees even when he wasn't standing.

Heat tore through him. He tightened his arms around her as his tongue danced with hers. He loved her taste almost as much he loved her scent, and he craved her with a hunger he felt all the way to his groin.

Channing's moans stirred sensual sensations all through him. They fed him. Stimulated him. Wildly intoxicated him. Nothing, and he meant nothing, was better than this—having your lips held captive by the woman you both loved and desired.

Her moans turned to whimpers when he deepened the kiss even more. Everything about her electrified him, made him feel whole and complete.

The sound of a car door slamming had him lifting his mouth off of hers. He stared at her, trying to come to terms with emotions that, until recently, had been foreign to him.

"What are you doing, Zane?" she asked in a slurred tone, as if she'd gotten tipsy from the intensity of the kiss.

"I was kissing you," he said smoothly. "And I want to kiss you some more. The Zane Westmoreland way."

He held her gaze. Saw the perceptive glint in her eyes. She knew just what a kiss *his way* entailed. Was she game? He was going to make sure that she was.

Lowering his mouth to hers, he kissed her again while wrapping her in his arms. This kiss was just as hot, just as greedy and just as intense, but this time it held more: doggedness, urgency.

Though it was hard to do so, he broke away from the kiss. He had to give her a choice. She could tell him to stop or give him the go-ahead. He watched as her expression got serious, her forehead knotted in deep consideration. He went still, not knowing what she'd decide, but knowing it was her decision to make. He would respect whatever it was.

He released a sigh of relief when she wrapped her arms around his neck, pressed her body close to his and tilted her mouth up to him. Grateful. Appreciative. Enthusiastic. He felt all of those things. Then he gently gathered her close, sliding his tongue between her lips.

He knew how much the kiss affected her when the arms around his neck tightened and her moans deepened and intensified. Her mouth was hot and delicious, and he was giving it one serious sensual assault. He wanted her. With a deep groan, he slowly lifted his head and kissed his way down her neck to the pulse throbbing at its side.

He pressed a lever that made both their seats glide back, and then, with the other hand, he adjusted the steering wheel out of their way. He pulled her into his lap, facing him. He felt the shivers that passed through her body when his teeth grazed across her skin.

She sucked in a deep breath when he whipped the tank top over her head and undid the front clasp of her bra. The minute he saw her breasts he lowered his lips to a nipple, greedily sucking it into his mouth. His hands were busy, unzipping her shorts and inching them—as well as her panties—down her thighs.

His mouth hungrily moved to the other breast while she moaned his name over and over. He raised her up as he worked his mouth down her naked body, licking her belly, tonguing her navel and then tilting his seat back in a reclining position so that Channing's feminine mound stared him in the face.

Craving her taste in a way he never had before, he grasped her thighs and slid his tongue inside. She sucked in a breath, and he sucked on her, fastening his mouth to her most sensitive spot with no intention of letting go until she screamed his name.

He held tight, needing this as much she did.

"Oh," Channing moaned as Zane's tongue made that swirling motion it could do so well. And then that same tongue began fluttering like crazy, sending all kinds of sensual vibrations ricocheting through her. Did he know how many nerve endings were located right here? Yes, oh, yes. Right there? Oh, yes, he knew. Zane knew just about everything when it came to a woman. And he was devouring her the way only he could.

He nibbled until she couldn't take any more. Spasms ripped into her body, making her scream. She trembled all over from head to toe and at the juncture of her thighs.

He wanted to be pushed, so she pushed. Boy, did she push, and he didn't let go. Didn't let up. And then she climaxed again. Her body became electrified all over again.

When the last sensation left her body, she moaned out his name and collapsed against him. He pulled his mouth away from her and gently eased her down his body. Then their mouths connected, and she tasted the essence of herself on his tongue.

She gripped his broad shoulders and felt his hard muscles. She pulled her mouth away and heard his deep masculine growl as he gathered her close and whispered, "Mine." At that moment, the possessive word didn't bother her like it should have.

With all the strength she could muster, she lifted her head to meet his gaze. Before she could say anything, he gave a tight yet gentle squeeze to her butt cheeks and said, "No. We didn't have sex. We shared a kiss."

Physically exhausted, she didn't have the strength to argue. And when he shifted their bodies so she could sit curled in his arms, she did, dropping her head on his chest, listening to the rapid beat of his heart against her cheek.

He held her and ran his hand all over her naked body as if stroking her to sleep. Zane's kisses were what erotic fantasies were made of, and he'd given her a double whammy. Orgasms like the ones she'd just had should be outlawed.

She yawned, feeling sleepy, and as she closed her eyes, too tired to keep them open, she heard him murmur something close to her ear, but she was too far gone to make out the words.

"I love you, baby."

Zane whispered the words although he doubted Channing heard what he said. She'd drifted asleep while naked in his arms.

He studied her features. They were peaceful, satisfied. Reaching into the backseat, he retrieved his jacket and placed it over her. A smile touched his lips as he thought about how she looked more *his* than ever.

He felt the rise and fall of her chest. He'd missed this, her falling asleep in his arms. But what he'd really missed was waking up with her draped over him, their legs entwined on those nights when he had stayed at her place or she had stayed at his. Upon waking, they would make love again. And again. His body hardened at the memories, and his erection poked her in the backside.

Zane noticed the movie screen. Although there was one more movie to be shown, a lot of people had already left. Half the number of cars filled the lot than there had been an hour ago. He glanced at the clock on the car's dashboard. Was it after midnight already? This was a weeknight. A number of people would have to be at work tomorrow.

In his mind, he tossed around plans for tomorrow. He didn't intend to let a single day go by without spending it with Channing. He would ask her to ride with him to Richmond.

She shifted in sleep, and the jacket covering her slid down an inch, exposing a plump breast and a juicy nipple. His mouth twitched, and the heat of desire rippled through him like a wave. The position wouldn't have been so bad if he wasn't inhaling her scent each and every time he took a breath.

Deciding he should take a quick nap as well, he closed his eyes and rested his chin on her forehead.

"Wake up, sleepyhead. Time for me to take you home."

Channing slowly opened her eyes and blinked a few times. Zane's face came into focus. She then gasped when she realized she was naked in his arms with only his jacket covering her. She scrambled to move from his lap, but Zane's hands tightened around her.

"Where do you think you're going?" he asked, his mouth quirking in a smile.

"I need to put on my clothes." She glanced out the window. The first thing she noticed was that the movie screen was black. The next was the absence of other cars. "Please don't tell me we're the last car here."

He chuckled. "Okay, I won't tell you."

"Zane!"

"Okay, we're not the last but pretty close. I will admit we're the only one on this row and the only vehicle that's still parked. Everyone else is leaving."

"Then give me my clothes."

"Hmm, the idea of driving you home with you wearing nothing is tempting."

She frowned. "Don't play with me, Zane. I need to get dressed before someone comes over here."

He smiled as he released her and watched her ease her panties up her legs and thighs before wiggling into them. The shorts were next. Then came the bra and tank top. He always liked watching her get dressed. As a doctor, she had to be prepared for any emergency, so she had a knack for dressing quickly when she needed to.

Channing glanced over at Zane while running her hands through her hair. "What are you looking at?"

"You."

"Shouldn't you start the ignition so we can leave?"

"In a minute." He leaned over and kissed her.

She frowned when he straightened and then started the car. His lips had been warm, and she could feel her bones turning to mush. Trying to ignore the way her belly was flipping all over the place, she asked, "What was that for?"

"I want you to dream about me tonight."

She drew in a deep breath. At least he hadn't suggested that he stay the night. Zane's kisses were always the prelude to something else. Specifically, the prelude to more intense lovemaking.

She didn't say anything because her head was already filled with memories of what had happened earlier. No sex but a degree of kissing only Zane could deliver. As she focused straight ahead, they left the drive-in theater, and she recalled how he had stripped her naked and feasted on her body. Why did the man have such a skillful mouth?

"I'm driving to Richmond this morning. You want to go with me?"

Channing glanced over at him. "Richmond?"

"Yes. Last year we sold a client in Richmond a couple of our horses, ones that I trained. I thought since I was in the area I would check on them. I talked to the guy yesterday, and he's all for it. In fact, he wants to talk to me about buying several more."

Channing stared at him. When they'd been together before, he would often tell her about his work, but there had never been a time when he'd invited her to go with him on any of his business trips. She'd always hoped he would ask.

"So will you go?"

"I had planned to spend time on the beach tomorrow."

"We can do that on Thursday."

Her forehead bunched. He was making plans for them to spend even more time together? "When are you going back to Denver?"

He shrugged. "It depends."

She lifted a brow. "On what?"

"You."

"Me?"

"Yes, you. I told you why I'm here."

"Yes, but I'll be staying in Virginia for another two weeks. Surely you don't plan to hang around here all that time."

He smiled over at her as he turned the corner into her beach community. "I don't see why not."

Her belly flipped again at the idea of him wanting to stay here in Virginia to be with her. "Don't you have work to do back in Denver?"

"Yes, but I'm doing some of it here using my laptop. I'm going through files and purging a number of accounts we've closed over the past year."

She knew how much he detested any sort of administrative work, yet he was doing it. So he could stay here with her. Zane preferred working outdoors with the horses. Did being with her mean that much to him? She shook her head, rejecting the notion.

"Channing? Ready for me to walk you to the door?"

She blinked upon realizing she was home already. When she opened the door, he grabbed the basket out of the backseat. They had finished off all the food, and the only things left in the basket were the wineglasses and wine bottle. "Keep these for whenever we finish off the rest of the wine."

She didn't say anything as she took the basket from him. He was beginning to sound sure of himself. Too sure of himself.

Channing would have walked quickly to the door, but he held her hand, deliberately slowing her pace. He didn't seem in any hurry, but she already had the key in her hand. "Thanks. Tonight was fun."

"Glad you enjoyed it, and about Richmond… You will take the drive with me, won't you?"

She swallowed as she tried to decide what she should do. "Yes, I'll go."

He smiled. "Great. I'll be here to pick you up around nine."

"All right."

He leaned in close and placed a gentle kiss on her cheek. "Need me to check inside before leaving?"

Channing shook her head as she opened the door. "No. I'll be fine."

"Okay. But how about giving me a sign after you get inside that everything's okay? I'm not moving the car until you do."

"Okay. Good night."

He smiled down at her. "Good night, Channing."

She closed the door, and after placing the basket in the kitchen, she went to the living room window and looked out. Zane's car was still in the driveway. She waved to him and watched him wave back before he backed out into the street.

She watched until he was no longer in sight. Then she went to the kitchen and pulled the wine bottle out of the basket, along with wineglasses. She poured wine into the glass that bore her name, thinking how pretty the glasses were and how thoughtful and touching it had been for Zane to buy them.

Taking her glass into the living room, she eased down on the sofa, fully aware of what tonight had done to her. It had pulled Zane deeper into her heart. She couldn't help but wonder if tonight had changed anything in his heart.

Probably not. She hadn't been the pusher this time but instead had been mainly a satisfied recipient. He had been the dominating male who took charge, and she had let him.

He needed to chill and let her handle things her way. Already he'd planned tomorrow for her, and if she let him, he would dominate the rest of her time in Virginia.

Channing suddenly realized that the one thing she'd never done before in their relationship was to take control. Whenever they'd made love, he'd been the one to initiate it.

Suddenly she had a plan.

"Not so fast, Zane Westmoreland," she muttered to herself. "Later today will be my time, and I intend to push you right off your feet."

Zane tossed his car keys on the table the moment he entered his suite, feeling good about his date with Channing. The look on her face as she'd stood at the window and waved goodbye had been priceless. His stomach had clenched tightly at the thought of actually driving away from her instead of staying the night to finish what they'd started at the drive-in.

It had been hard to keep driving without making a U-turn back to her. But she had set the "no sex" rule, and he'd given his word that he would adhere to her wishes. But like he had shown her tonight, he had no qualms about stretching the limits of that rule to his advantage whenever he could.

He was about to toss his jacket across the chair when his cell phone rang. Pulling it out of his jacket pocket, he gritted back a curse. It was Megan. A part of him didn't want to answer it, but with his luck, she would call Channing next and he definitely didn't want that. He didn't need Megan sticking her nose where it didn't belong. How he and Channing decided to work things out was no business of his sister's.

He clicked on the phone. "What do you want, Megan? It's late."

"I know what time it is, Zane. I had emergency surgery at the hospital and I'm on my way home. I also know where you are."

"And?" He braced himself for his sister's tirade. Since marrying Rico, his emotionally detached sister had been showing all kinds of emotion. She'd become expressive as hell, and for someone who'd once prided herself on having self-control, the new Megan took a lot of getting used to.

"I'm glad you've come to your senses."

He raised a brow. "Meaning?"

"Meaning, I talked to Channing yesterday, and I believe it."

He paused to lean in the doorway that separated the sitting area from the bedroom. "Believe what, Megan?"

"That you finally realize you love her."

Zane let out a relieved breath. At least his sister believed him. Too bad the woman he loved wasn't there yet. "What made you change your mind?"

"You would not have lied to Rico. You had no reason to do so. And then you dropped everything to fly out there to plead your case and surrender your heart."

"Yeah, for all the good it's doing," he said, suddenly feeling frustrated. He was glad his sister didn't consider his actions suspect, but he still had his work cut out for him. Channing wasn't making things easy for him.

"Don't give up, Zane. You hurt her, and she has to learn to trust you again. You have to give her a reason to believe in you. She has to know that she can win your heart fair and square."

"She's won my heart already, Megan. I love her. But she doesn't believe me because I made the mistake of telling her so many times that I *didn't* love her."

"Um, like the boy who cried wolf. He cried it so long that when the real wolf came along, no one wanted to believe him."

"I know, and I only have myself to blame."

"Well, we're all rooting for you."

He chuckled. "We?"

"Yes, the entire Westmoreland clan. At least those of us who understand what true love is about. After loving Rico, I can't imagine a person not being with the one person who has their heart. The one person they know will make them happy."

Less than an hour later, when Zane eased into bed and slid between the sheets, he thought of his conversation with Megan. He was grateful that she believed him. Now he had to make Channing believe.

He smiled, thinking that in a few hours he intended to turn up the heat.

Eleven

"Ready?"

Channing blinked at the sensations twirling around in her stomach.

They could have been caused by the deep, husky timbre of Zane's voice or by the way he leaned in her doorway, dressed in a pair of jeans and a chambray shirt, with his Stetson riding low on his head. His navigator sunglasses finished off the package, and she was convinced he was the most handsome man she'd ever seen.

Why did his smile seem so luscious and sexy this morning?

"Yes, I'm ready. Come on in," she said, stepping aside. "I just need to grab my purse. I figure we can come back here later and eat dinner. I still have a lot of leftovers."

He took off his sunglasses. She could tell he was surprised by her invitation. "All right. Sounds like a plan to me."

She was about to walk off to get her purse when he touched her arm. "Not so fast." He pulled her into his arms and let his gaze move up and down her body. "You look pretty."

"Thanks." She had taken great pains to look nice today. From the appreciative look in his eyes, she knew it was worth it. His desire caused goose bumps to form on her arms. "And you look nice yourself."

They stood for a moment, staring at each other. Channing could feel the heat and the charged air between them. She couldn't help but remember what had happened last night at the drive-in. Those same memories were what had kept her up most of the night as primal needs ripped through her.

She absently licked her lips and heard Zane's breath catch. "What's wrong?" she asked.

Instead of answering, he held her gaze. She felt the fire in every part of her body.

"Nothing's wrong, baby. In fact, everything is right." He drew her close and lowered his mouth to hers.

If he thought she would resist, he was wrong. Channing even stretched up on tiptoe to meet his mouth. His hands went around her waist, and she grabbed his massive shoulders, pressing her body against perfect abs and muscular thighs.

But what made her breasts throb was the engorged bulge pressing hard at the juncture of her thighs.

If he needed to be pushed, then she would push with all the strength she could muster.

She hoped she wasn't making a mistake.

Nothing, and she meant nothing, was better than the way Zane's mouth mated with hers. He relished her with a hunger that made her moan deep in her throat and made her wet between her legs simultaneously. A sense of intimacy that she'd fought for the past day overtook her, had her needing sexual fulfillment as much as she needed her next breath.

When her body began to quiver, he slowly pulled his mouth away and stood holding her until the last shiver left her body. As if to satisfy her one last time, he licked his tongue across her lips before nibbling the corners of her mouth with his teeth. Tingles swept through her.

"If we don't leave now, we'll never get out of here," he whispered against her lips. "My self-control is slipping, and I'm tempted to say to hell with your 'no sex' rule, lift up this sundress and ease inside of you."

She could imagine it happening. Her body was ready, aching for the feel of his shaft thrusting in and out of her. She was intensely aroused and knew there was no way he hadn't realized it. He was very acute when it came to that.

"Um," she said, backing out of his arms. She needed to put some space between them. "Excuse me for a minute."

"Take your time. I'm not going anywhere."

She moved toward her bedroom, but before opening the door and stepping inside, she paused and glanced over her shoulder. He stood there, looking so incredibly sexy that the sight was an assault on her senses in every way.

"If you prefer that we spend the day here doing nothing, our plans can be changed, Channing."

She was tempted. Boy, was she tempted. But she wanted to go with him to Richmond and do something with him she'd never done before… She wanted to see a part of his life he'd kept from her. "No. I'm looking forward to going to Richmond with you."

"All right."

Lust surrounded them, but she was determined to change all that lust into love. More than anything, she wanted to believe that she could.

"Need my help, Channing?"

She blinked upon realizing that she'd been standing there staring at him like a dimwit. She had wanted to change into new underwear, a special pair just right for the heat building between them. Suddenly, she could see him kneeling before her and easing her panties down her legs, helping her into a new, lacy pair. She opened her mouth to tell him that she didn't need his help but then decided it was time she tested his control.

"If you like."

She saw the heat that flared in his eyes. "Yes, I would definitely like."

Channing nodded before continuing to her bedroom, and he followed. She moved to the dresser and pulled out a pair of black lace panties. She held up several. She knew that was his preference.

A smile curved his lips.

She closed the drawer and brought the pair of undies to him. He took them from her fingers and slowly knelt down in front of her. Reaching out, he ran his calloused hands up her dress and between her legs. The contact with her skin had blood rushing through her veins.

Channing met the dark, heavy-lidded eyes gazing up at her, saw how his control was being stretched. His jaw clenched tight, and his nostrils flared while he eased her plain panties down her legs. She could hear the intensity of his breathing, and her breasts felt tight. When her panties were down to her knees, his hand paused, and then heated fingers inched back up between her legs to caress the folds of her womanhood. She drew in a quick breath when he slid two fingers inside of her.

"Zane…" His name eased from her lips. An intense desire stirred in the pit of her stomach when he stroked her. Automatically, her inner muscles clenched as his fingers gave her a sensuous workout. Then, as if he'd merely wanted to remind her of what gifted fingers he had, he withdrew his touch. She watched as he took those same fingers, wet with her moisture from her body, and inserted them into his mouth. He sucked hard, as if relishing the taste of her nectar.

Watching him made her weak in the knees, but before she could sink to the floor, he returned his hand to her thighs to complete the task of removing her panties. He was slow, taking his time, and the feel of the skimpy fabric easing down her legs set off primitive urges within her. The eyes staring up at her held such a fierce hunger in their dark depths that she felt drawn to him more than ever before.

"You can step out of them now."

His words floated up to her, and she lifted her legs to step out of her panties. Her breath lodged in her throat when he took the fresh pair from her and slid them up her legs. He rubbed his face against her thighs before inhaling deeply.

"I'm convinced I'm addicted to this," he said. "It always amazed me how wet you can get for me," he said, his dark eyes glinting with heated lust.

It always amazed her, as well. When he lifted her dress and took his hot tongue and drew a circle around her navel before pulling her panties the rest of the way up, she swore she felt the floor shake beneath her feet.

Sensations swamped her. When he stood and gave her backside a playful smack, those sensations vibrated something fierce, sending tremors running through her.

"Anything else you need help with before we leave?"

She took a step back and eased down her dress. "No, that's it. I would not have wanted to change my underwear if you hadn't kissed me the way you did."

He chuckled. "Do you want me to promise not to kiss you again?"

She thought about his question and immediately knew the answer. "No, that's not what I want."

Zane stared at her intently, and she felt his uncensored look. "Good, because I doubt I could do that, anyway." He reached out and took her hand. "Come on, baby, let's go."

Sipping the beer Morris Holder had given him, Zane thought the same thing now that he had thought last year when he, Derringer and Jason had met with the man. This was a pretty nice spread. But as far as he was concerned, nothing was more beautiful than Westmoreland land, and he had a special affection for Zane's Hideout. His spread was the best with the lake and the mountains surrounding it. Now that Bailey's spread was next to his, he wondered if Ramsey and Dillon meant to punish him when they'd given her that parcel. Lord, help him. At least it was still undeveloped land, and Bailey wasn't showing any interest in building anything on it.

Instead of taking the interstate, he had driven the scenic route to Richmond, making various stops along the way and enjoying lunch at a café in Jamestown. What would normally have taken two hours had taken more than three, but he hadn't wanted to hurry. He preferred spending quality time with Channing.

Turning his thoughts back to Morris, Zane took another sip of beer. A self-made billionaire at fifty-eight, Morris was in great physical shape. He had his own workout room with every piece of exercise equipment imaginable. And then there was his stable of horses, which Zane knew Morris rode often.

Zane moved his gaze to the view of the meadows, and his stomach clenched when he saw Channing. She was walking beside Morris's wife, Lisa. Lisa was a beauty in her own right, but no one, he thought, was more beautiful than Channing. He loved her yellow sundress. It looked damn good on her. Sexy.

"Channing's a nice woman, Zane."

He glanced back at Morris. "Thanks."

"Any plans for the future?"

Zane wasn't surprised by the man's question. The last time he was here, Morris had been a bachelor for more than twenty years, and Lisa had been his live-in lover. Now the two were married. "Yes, I plan to marry her as soon as I can convince her that I love her."

Morris nodded. "Good luck, and don't give up. I woke up one morning and decided I had been a single man long enough. Over breakfast, I asked Lisa to marry me. For the longest time, she thought I wasn't serious because I'd never mentioned marriage before. There was the issue of the twenty-five-year difference in our ages. That issue used to concern me, but on that morning, it no longer did. Age is nothing more than a number, and I refused to go another day without making plans for a future with the woman I loved and cared about most."

Zane nodded and took another sip of beer. "She didn't have a problem with your sudden change of heart?"

He chuckled. "Not sure she had a problem with it, but she was skeptical at first. The subject of marriage had never come up between us, so I think she thought I was dying or something. Convincing her that I wasn't was hard, but I did it."

Morris took a sip of his own beer and then added,

"Women don't understand that men might be slow, but when we make up our minds about something, that's it."

Zane released a deep breath. "Yeah, that's it."

But it seemed he was having a harder time convincing Channing than Morris had convincing Lisa. A small smile stretched across his mouth. He wouldn't give up.

Morris stood. "Lisa and I would certainly love it if you and Channing stayed and had dinner with us."

Zane stood as well, an appreciative smile touched his lips. "Thanks for the invite, but Channing and I have made dinner plans already."

What he wasn't saying was that he couldn't wait to get back to Channing's grandparents' home to be alone with her.

"I like Lisa. Did you know she used to be a pharmacist? That's how she and Morris met," Channing said. "He happened to drop by the drugstore where she was working one day."

She and Zane had left Richmond and were on their way back to Virginia Beach. While Zane and Morris had talked business, she and Lisa had gotten to know each other, and Lisa had given Channing a tour of their beautiful ranch. Lisa had also told her about the twenty-five-year age difference between her and Morris.

Channing had been surprised when Lisa had said she and Morris had been married only a little more than a year after being lovers for five years. Five years! It was hard to believe that Lisa had been willing to wait five years for Morris's affections. Channing had bolted from Zane after nine months, telling herself that had been long enough.

"Yes, Lisa is a nice person, and Morris did mention how they met."

Channing's gaze shifted to look out the car window. Lisa and Morris's story was something Channing couldn't get out of her mind. She shifted her gaze back to Zane. He was hot, and she could feel the heat radiating from his body to hers. His eyes, hidden behind his sunglasses, were on the road, which was fine since she wanted to watch him.

There was no way she could have remained Zane's lover for five years without knowing for certain how he felt about her. Her makeup was totally different from Lisa's. Her parents and grandparents had always claimed she had a low tolerance for some things, that she lacked patience. She wondered if her impatience had worked against her where Zane was concerned.

They came to a stop at a traffic light, and she could feel the dark depths of Zane's eyes staring back at her behind his sunglasses. Her heart thumped hard in her chest, and her breath stopped from the intensity of his gaze.

"Is anything wrong, Channing?" he asked her.

"No, but I have a question for you. Lisa and Morris were lovers for five years before Morris asked her to marry him. Had I not left Denver for Atlanta when I did…had I remained there as your lover, where would we be now?"

She watched as a frown of concentration marred his forehead. "I honestly don't know," he said softly. "I want to think I would have come to my senses and you and I would be married, or at least engaged. But I can't rightly say. It took your leaving a second time to make me realize what you meant to me."

Channing nodded. *What she meant to him…* Even now she wasn't sure what that was and had only a limited amount of time to find out.

The car moved again, and Zane shifted his gaze back to the road. Behind the sunglasses, he tried to keep his eyes from blazing in frustration. When would she ever believe that he actually loved her? What if she never believed it?

For the first time in his life, he was dealing with the fear of losing the woman he loved. The thought that no matter how hard he tried he could still end up without her as his wife sent a rush of irritation flowing all through him.

Hey, don't even think of losing her, man. You got yourself in this mess, and you can get yourself out. You got to make her feel as if she's the most important person in the world to you, because she is.

He brought the car to a stop again at another traffic light. He glanced over at Channing to find her still looking at him, and he drew in a shaky breath. The air between them was charged.

She absently licked her lips and tucked strands of her windblown hair behind her ear. At that moment, all he could think about was just how delicious the area around her ear tasted. He'd used his tongue there a number of times.

He was a man with a healthy sexual appetite, but he knew she equated his desire with lust. How could he get her to understand that his sexual need for her was an extension of his love? He was fully aware she was fighting her own deep attraction to him.

"Got any plans when we get back to your place?" he asked when traffic began moving again.

She shrugged. "I thought I'd grab something out of the freezer for a quick meal and then I'll let you come up with ideas for ways to spend the rest of the day."

He wasn't so sure she would want to do that. If she

left it up to him, they would be making love all over the place for the rest of the day and well into the night. "I guess we can spend time on the beach," he offered.

"Yes, I guess we can do that."

When traffic slowed up again, he gave a quick glance over to her. She hadn't sounded enthused about doing that. "Any other ideas?" he asked holding her gaze.

"Anything you want to do is fine with me, Zane."

His erection began throbbing again. He quirked an eyebrow at her to make sure they were on the same page. "Anything?"

"Yes, *anything.*"

Shivers of anticipation raced through his body, and he broke eye contact with her to return his gaze to the road. If she thought he didn't intend to hold her to what she'd just said, she had another thought coming.

He glanced at the clock on the car's console. At that moment, he decided to discontinue driving the scenic route and hit the interstate. She had been sending out some pretty strong vibes today, vibes that all but declared that she was now in the driver's seat. And he couldn't get back to Kindle Shores quick enough to find out just how she would drive him over the edge.

Channing watched the endless stretch of two-lane road ahead of them. She'd told Zane what she wanted, and knowing him like she did, he would take full advantage of it.

And she'd be ready when he did.

Her body had been attuned to him since he'd changed her panties that morning. At the Holders' ranch, she had caught him staring at her more than once, pinning her with his dark gaze. Other than when Lisa had invited her to take a tour of the ranch so Morris and Zane could talk business, he had been there by Channing's side.

She had been fully aware of him every time his arm had snaked around her waist, every time he'd taken her hand in his, every time he'd brushed a wayward curl back from her face. Those looks and impromptu touches had ignited a flame inside her, one she hadn't been able to put out yet. So here she was, probably as aroused as Zane, and it didn't matter that he knew it.

"Did skipping out on that symposium cause problems for you at the hospital, Channing?"

She looked at him, finding it oddly gratifying that he cared. "No. I have a really good relationship with Dr. Rowe and the other top hospital administrators. I had only committed myself for three weeks, although I'd taken a six-week leave from my position in Atlanta."

"But you would have considered staying all six weeks."

She noted he said it as a statement more than a question. She could tell him that she had been leaning toward not doing the additional three weeks because being back in the same town with him hadn't been easy. She had even considered visiting her brother and his family in San Diego for a week or so. But Zane didn't need to know any of that.

"Maybe. Maybe not," she said. "I hadn't made up my mind yet."

"But what happened at McKays that night made you decide to leave."

Again, he had presented it as a statement. "Yes," she said. "It helped me to decide."

"I'm sorry I drove you away from Denver. But I'm not sorry for coming after you, and I'll do so again if I have to, Channing. To be quite honest, my real mistake was not coming after you that first time."

His words gave her pause and reminded her that the Zane she'd known had been quite the ladies' man. He would have no reason to run behind any woman, no matter how much she had wanted to be his exception.

"Just think how different things would be now if I had come after you," he added.

Channing smiled at him. "And how different do you think things would be, Zane?" she asked and noticed he was pulling off to the side of the road.

Zane brought the car to a stop, cut the engine and turned to her. "I want to think we'd be married with a baby."

"A baby?"

Seeing the startled look on her face, a smile curved his lips. "Yes, Channing. A baby. My baby. Don't you like children?"

"Yes, but..."

"But what?"

"We never discussed children," she said softly.

No, he thought, they hadn't. Mainly because he'd never wanted to discuss a future with her. "We're talking about them now."

"Are we?"

"Yes. I like kids. What about you?"

She nodded. "Yes, I like them."

"How many do you want us to have?" he asked her. "I want several since I'm used to a big family. Hey, we can be like my cousin Quade and have three in one day."

Channing's mouth dropped open, and she simply stared at him. She knew all about Quade's babies. Triplets. "Are you crazy?"

He chuckled. "Yes, I am. I'm crazy about you." He

brushed a kiss across her lips. "If you don't want triplets, I'll settle for twins."

Zane laughed at her shocked expression as he
straightened in his seat. Turning the car's ignition back
on, he maneuvered the vehicle onto the road knowing
he'd given Channing something to think about.

Channing didn't say anything as she watched Zane
switch from the two-lane road and take the ramp that led
to the interstate. What *could* she say when her mind was
spinning? Zane had just implied they had a future. With
children. She wasn't mistaken about that. She knew he
liked children. She'd seen him around his cousin Dillon's son. But Zane had never brought up the subject of
children they would have together.

But today he had.

Channing stole another glance at Zane. She had
to admit that over the past two days she had detected
changes in him. Positive changes. He wasn't as in-
flexible as he once had been, and he came off as less
guarded. He was letting her into his private world.
A small stirring of pleasure rippled through her and
warmed her insides. They were making progress.

A good twenty minutes or more passed. When she
saw they were taking the exit for Kindle Shores, anticipation nipped at her heels. Although Zane's expression was well hidden by those navigator sunglasses,
she knew he was just as eager as she was to get to their
destination.

Within five minutes, Zane pulled the car into her
driveway as all kinds of emotions churned inside of
her. As he cut off the engine, she saw his fingers tap
the steering wheel while he focused desire-drenched
eyes on her.

"Are you hungry?" he asked in a low, sensuous tone.

His question had a mouthwatering effect…but it wasn't for food. "No. You?" The sun was shining brightly overhead, but Channing knew that wasn't the reason the interior of the car felt so hot.

"A meal isn't what I have an intense hunger for now, Channing."

Her breath caught. His words, spoken in a quiet voice, compelled every single cell in her body to ignite in an overaroused state.

She swallowed. "And what is it that you want?"

His fingers stopped tapping the steering wheel. Instead, those fingers brushed across her wrist, making every erogenous zone in her body come alive with a need she couldn't deny.

Holding her gaze, he leaned toward her and whispered, "I want you every way I can have you."

Channing felt as though every nerve in her body was on fire. She drew in a deep breath. "Then maybe we need to take this inside."

A sexy smile touched his lips. "I agree."

Twelve

No sooner had the door closed behind them, Zane and Channing were tearing off each other's clothes. Zane knew wanting any woman this much had to be insane, but that thought was wiped from his brain with the erotic sweep of her tongue in his mouth. Where had this intense hunger come from? How was it driving him as much as it was driving her?

She had him pinned against the door and was pushing him to do anything she wanted. He was definitely game as long as she kept kissing him this way, so deeply and completely. When she suddenly jerked her mouth free, dropped to her knees in front of him and took his engorged sex into her hands, he groaned deep in his throat.

"Ah, hell!" He threw his head back as her heated tongue swirled over his swollen shaft before she hungrily mouthed the full length of him. He groaned when suddenly it seemed as if she would swallow him whole. She was using her mouth to infuse her ownership on this part of him. And she was doing so in the most earth-shattering way known to man.

Pleasure shot to all parts of his body. She was building a fire within him and quenching it at the same time.

While her fingertips stroked his thatch of curly hair, her mouth sucked harder. Then her fingers shifted lower to gently squeeze his testicles, causing a jolt of pleasure to tear through him. Did she know her actions were the embodiment of his wet dreams? Did she know she was bonding herself to him?

He grabbed her head, twining his fingers through the silky strands of her hair before wrapping a lock around his fist to hold her mouth right there. Yes, oh, yes. Right. There. And then he felt it, the first vibrations stirring in his groin.

"Channing," he whispered as sensations flooded through him. His heart was racing, and he couldn't get his breathing regulated. And then with one brutal yet erotic suck of her mouth, the intensity slammed into him. He felt the release gush into her mouth.

There weren't any words that could define what he felt at that moment. Though *mind-blowing* was close. He groaned her name over and over until the last sensation had swept through his body.

He didn't recall when she let go of him or when she eased to her feet. All he remembered was gazing through a haze of sensuous contentment to stare into the depths of her eyes.

"Channing—"

He wanted to tell her he loved her. But before he could fix his mouth to say the words, her soft lips took

control of his, and she kissed him with such complete-
ness it had him groaning out loud again.

He couldn't take any more. He swept her off her feet,
into his arms, and headed for the bedroom.

When Zane placed her on the bed, Channing stared
up at him, watching the intensity in his features. She
had a feeling this lovemaking would be different from
any other they'd shared. When he joined her in bed,
her legs automatically opened for him. With the ease
of a man who knew just what he wanted, Zane slid between them.

They stared at each other for several heartbeats before she felt him filling her with long, powerful thrusts,
stretching her and going deep. When he continued moving in and out in long, languorous strokes, the rhythm
caused electrifying sensations to overtake her. His
hands tightened on her hips, holding her immobile while
he totally possessed her feminine core.

"Ah," she groaned while intense pleasure blazed
through every part of her.

Then his strokes became harder and harder, deeper
and deeper, complete and absolute. The result was stag-
geringly powerful.

She met his gaze, and the look in his eyes took her
breath away. For the first time in her life, she felt an
emotion coming from him that she'd never felt before. It
might have been a figment of her imagination or wish-
ful thinking, but she decided to take the feeling and
run with it.

The moment that decision was made, her body
seemed to splinter into a thousand pieces. She dug her
fingers into his shoulders, and it was only then that he

lowered his head and took her mouth to drown out her screams.

When he withdrew from the kiss, he whispered against her lips, "That was lovemaking, *not* sex. It's never been just sex with you, Channing. Never."

Then he grasped her face in both hands and lowered his mouth to kiss her again. Channing doubted she could ever love him any more than she did at that moment.

"I'm glad you haven't lost your touch in the kitchen, Channing."

Channing smiled at Zane while placing a plate of cookies in front of him as he sat at the kitchen table. She slid into the chair across from him. "And I'm glad you haven't lost your touch in the bedroom."

At his deep chuckle, she grabbed one of the cookies and bit into it. They had made love several times before finally getting out of bed and putting on clothes... at least some of them. He had slid into his jeans and she into his shirt. Then they had gone into the kitchen to get something to eat.

Channing had taken a few things out of the freezer before they'd left for Richmond, and all she had to do was place them in the microwave. Now she and Zane were sitting at the table enjoying cookies and milk for dessert. It seemed all the dishes she'd prepared during her cooking frenzy were his favorites. Go figure.

When she saw the way he was looking at her, she took a deep, quivering breath. It didn't help matters that he was shirtless with that powerful chest on display. A chest she had licked all over hours ago. She shivered at the memory. Lord! She needed a cold glass of water. Quick. The glass of milk just wasn't doing it.

"Excuse me," she said, getting up from the table. She strolled over to the refrigerator to get a chilled bottle of water. She quickly opened the refrigerator, grabbed one, unscrewed the top and took a huge gulp, appreciating how the cold liquid flowed down her throat. Boy, she'd needed that.

"You want to share?"

She jumped. She hadn't known Zane had gotten out of his chair and was standing right there in front of her. "Sure," she said, reaching behind her to reopen the refrigerator.

"No, I want to share yours."

"Oh." She handed him her bottle and watched him finish it off before he placed it on the counter.

He then smiled at her and said, "You make me hot, baby."

Her insides stirred. If he only knew how hot he made her. She raised her palm to his forehead. "Um, you feel normal."

His lips curved in a smile as he took hold of her hand and lowered it to his zipper. "Can you say the same here?" he asked.

She swallowed. No, she couldn't. He felt huge, engorged and erect. You would think that with as much action as they'd had earlier, more sex would be the last thing on their minds. Evidently not.

"Well?"

She cupped him through his jeans and watched desire flare in his eyes. "I can handle this."

"You're the only woman who can," he said throatily, reaching up to peel his shirt off her. "So tell me, Channing Hastings," he said, tugging out of his jeans, "have you ever been taken against a refrigerator?"

"No." She breathed the words. Blood rushed thickly

through her veins at the thought of such a thing happening.

He lifted her, and her legs automatically wrapped around his waist. "Then consider this your first time… but it won't be your last, baby."

Zane lay awake, staring at the ceiling, while a naked Channing slept soundly beside him. Something flared deep within him when he thought about how they had spent their day, beginning with the drive to Richmond and then returning here.

It reminded him of how things used to be on her free days from the hospital. She would spend her time with him at the Hideout. How could he not have seen then just how great they were together? Although he'd known their relationship was good, he hadn't understood the significance of what that meant until it was too late. That was why he was here backpedaling, trying to convince her that he loved her, doing whatever it took to get that message across.

After they'd made love in the kitchen, starting out against the refrigerator and ending up on the counter, they had dressed and taken a walk on the beach. They had run into Ronald and his family. Zane had been introduced to Jennifer and their two kids. Seeing Ronald with his family made Zane long for that same thing with Channing. He'd meant what he'd told her yesterday. He wanted kids and looked forward to the children they would make together.

When they'd returned to her villa, he'd hinted that he needed to go back to the hotel to change clothes. He had hoped she would suggest he check out of the hotel altogether and spend the rest of his time at the beach house with her. But she hadn't. He'd been disappointed, but he hadn't pushed. He recalled one of his father's old sayings: "Anything worth getting is worth waiting for...." And he knew deep in his heart that Channing was worth waiting for. He was determined to rid her of any and all doubt about his love for her.

She shifted her body in sleep, and immediately he became aroused. When he felt her hand on his thigh, every cell in his body became energized. She slowly opened her eyes, and his heart pounded in his chest when she smiled at him.

"Now that you're awake," he said softly, brushing hair from her face, "I need to leave."

"To go back to the hotel?" she asked quietly.

"Yes."

He saw the slight marring of her forehead and knew she was trying to make a decision. When she shifted closer and eased her thigh between his, he knew she had made it.

"Since you're determined for me to push you into falling in love with me, then maybe you should stay here."

He cupped her chin in his hand. "You sure? Whether I stay here or at the hotel, I'm not leaving Virginia Beach until you do, Channing."

She nodded. "I'm sure. So unless you're desperate for your things, you can wait until the morning to go get them."

His hand left her chin to rub his own. "I can use a shave, but I can wait until tomorrow. If you wake up in the morning and I'm not here, that's where I'll be... checking out of the hotel."

"All right."

He kissed her and felt that special connection between them. They still had more road to travel, but at that moment, he felt that they were at least making progress.

The ringing of the telephone woke Channing. She noticed the spot beside her in bed was empty as she reached for her cell phone on the nightstand. "Hello," she said in a sleepy tone.

"Gracious. You're still in bed?"

Channing came wide-awake upon hearing her grandmother's voice. She glanced over at the clock. It was close to eleven. Typically she was an early riser, but when you spent most of the night making love, exhaustion had a tendency to creep up on you.

"Yes, I'm still in bed. How are you Gramma?"

"I'm fine, but I wanted to check on you. Our last conversation had me worried."

Channing took a deep breath. "I know, but I'm better."

"Does that mean your opinion of men is better?"

Channing thought of the past two days she'd spent with Zane and how thoughtful and considerate he'd been. But, most importantly, she thought of how he'd included her in his world. "Yes, it's improved some."

"Glad to hear it."

She and her grandmother talked for a little while longer before they ended their call. Channing stretched and then eased out of bed. Thinking of Zane checking out of the hotel, she nibbled her bottom lip. She wanted to be optimistic that she wasn't making a mistake.

She hoped she wasn't wrong, but she was beginning to feel a special bond between them, and it wasn't just about sex…although she thought that part of their relationship was super, too. She felt more.

But then, she quickly reminded herself, she had felt more the last time they'd been together, when she'd assumed he had fallen in love with her. She couldn't afford to make another mistake about something like that. So she would take one day at a time. She wouldn't rush, but she would, in her own way, continue to push him. Yes, she'd push, but she wouldn't shove. In her mind, there was a difference. If he was close, she would see to it that he got closer. She had to believe that Zane was worth taking a chance on.

The sound of a car door closing had her looking out the window. Zane was back, and she watched as he went to the trunk of the car and removed his luggage and laptop. As if he felt her watching, he glanced at the window, tilted his Stetson back and looked straight at her. When he smiled, she actually felt it radiate from him to her and she smiled back. Then he did something that the Zane she'd always known would never have done.

He blew her a kiss.

Her breath caught, and his gesture sent a warm rush of pleasure flowing through her. This was the man she loved, the man she wanted to marry and the man she wanted as a father for her children.

Suddenly, she realized that she was looking at the world through rose-colored glasses again, and Zane had once again unlocked her heart.

Thirteen

"Zane, don't you dare! Put me down this instant!"

"Okay."

And he did so, unceremoniously dumping her into the ocean. Channing surfaced, sputtering and pushing wet hair from her face. "How dare you!"

"I dare because I thought you needed cooling off. I saw the way you were looking at me. Like you wanted to jump my bones."

"I was not, you arrogant, conceited...!"

Ignoring her ravings, he continued. "Not that I'm complaining about you wanting a little roll in the sand. But although this is considered a private beach, there are others around. What would the Farmers think? Or your grandparents' neighbors for that matter?"

Instead of answering, she shot him a venomous look before turning to swim the short distance back to shore. He let her go. There was no doubt in his mind that she was angry with him. He smiled, thinking he would have to make up with her. The thought fired his blood. Making up with Channing was always an enjoyable experience.

Since he was in the water, he might as well take a leisurely swim. Because there were so many lakes on Westmoreland land, the one thing his parents had been sure to teach their offspring was how to swim. He considered himself pretty good at it...mainly because of the swimming races he, his brothers and his cousins had held during the summer months while growing up. He'd been the reigning champ for years...until Bailey showed him up. Now the little nymph still held the title.

He glanced to where Channing lay on the towel she had stretched out on the sand. It was hard to believe it had been a week since he'd moved out of the hotel. As far as he was concerned, every day seemed like heaven.

They woke up making love and went to bed making love. In between, they spent the day on the beach or, like yesterday, shopped. She had been determined that he should purchase a pair of shorts, and, to satisfy her, he had. After she had whistled outrageously about what a nice pair of legs he had, he'd poked out his chest and decided wearing the damn things wouldn't be so bad... especially if it meant she would continue looking at him with all that sexual hunger in her eyes.

After spending enough time in the water, he swam back to shore. Smiling, he sauntered across the beautiful white sand toward Channing. She opened her eyes and eased up when she heard his approach.

"Relax, I'm not going to bother you," he said, flopping down on the towel beside her.

She frowned over at him. "You better not."

He pretended to shiver. "Now I'm scared," he teased.

She rolled her eyes and lay back down. "Your cell phone's been ringing," she said casually, although he knew there was nothing casual about it. A lot of women had his number, and being missing in action probably had a lot of them worried about him. Evidently, no one in his family was giving out information as to his whereabouts so the women had taken to calling. For the past couple of days, he had turned off his phone. He'd cut it back on this morning to check with his family and to call the phone company to request a new phone number. The latter was something he hadn't told her about yet.

"It was someone in my family," he said, looking over at her.

She frowned. "You have *several* missed calls, Zane."

"Like I said, it's someone in my family," he said, reaching out and sweeping a lock of damp hair from her face.

"How can you be so sure?"

A smile ruffled his mouth. "Because I had my number changed this morning. No one has it but my family, and they wouldn't share it without my permission."

He saw the surprised look on her face. "You had your number changed?"

"Yes, and you're the only woman who's not related to me who has it."

She gave him another surprised look. "I have it?"

He nodded. "Yes. I keyed it into your phone while you were washing your hair this morning."

"Oh." She didn't say anything for a minute, but he knew the idea of him having a new, private phone number pleased her. He was glad that it did.

"And speaking of my hair, I'm going to have to wash it again, thanks to you."

"No problem, I'll help." He saw the way her cheeks flushed at his offer. No doubt she was remembering what had happened when he'd offered to help wash her hair the last time, three days ago.

He reached over and pulled his cell phone out of the shorts he had left on the chaise longue with his shirt. He checked the missed calls. "Canyon. Canyon. Canyon. Canyon and Canyon," he said, grinning. "I told you."

"Sounds like he needs to talk to you," Channing said.

Zane shrugged. "He has woman issues."

"And you being *Dear Zane* like *Dear Abby* will help him solve his problem, right?"

He chuckled. "Kinda. Sorta." Then he held her gaze and said in a serious tone, "I know about women, yes. But with the one woman I should have known about and should have handled with the love and respect she deserved, I blew it."

He watched as his words gave her pause. His heart pounded when she only smiled. He didn't say anything, either. He wanted to let her think about what he'd just said.

"You want to go to the drive-in movies again tonight?" he asked her a short while later.

"Um, what's playing?"

He chuckled. "Does it matter?" They had gone to the drive-in two other times and had totally enjoyed making out in the car.

She smiled over at him. "No, it doesn't matter, and yes, I'd love to go to the drive-in with you tonight."

"What do you want, Canyon?" Zane asked his cousin later that evening. He and Channing had enjoyed their time on the beach. Then, like he said he would, he had helped wash her hair…which led to other things. They had eaten dinner, and Channing had gone next door to give the Farmers a batch of the cookies she'd baked earlier that day.

"I can't believe you're just calling me back, Zane. I could have been dying," Canyon snapped.

Zane rolled his eyes. "You're talking to me now so you're not dead. What do you want?"

"Keisha. I told her we should talk, but she says she doesn't want to have anything to do with me."

Zane glanced at his watch. He couldn't wait to go to the movies with Channing. "Either take her at her word or do something about it. Action speaks louder than words."

"I guess you would know. Word has it that you're somewhere trying to convince Channing you're falling in love with her."

Zane heard the smirk in Canyon's voice. "For your damn information, Canyon, I'm not falling in love with Channing. I just told her that."

Channing had returned from next door and walked toward the bedroom to let Zane know she was back when the words he'd blared out to his cousin stopped her. Her head spun in shock at what he'd just said.

He was not falling in love with her?

He had lied to her?

Her body quivered in pain. He had been playing a game with her all along. A game with her heart.

Not able to handle what she was feeling, she turned, nearly blinded by her tears, and rushed back out of the house.

"What do you mean you just told her that?" Canyon asked. "Megan and Bailey are convinced you're crazy about Channing and told us not to be surprised if you came back married."

Not a bad idea, Zane thought, and knew he would give it more consideration later. "The reason I'm not falling in love with Channing is because I'm already in love with her. I realized just how much I loved her before I left Denver. But she doesn't believe me. And I'm here to prove otherwise."

Canyon didn't say anything for a long moment. "So it's true. Some woman has finally gotten to you?"

Zane smiled. "Yes. The same way a woman got to you, and once they get to you, Canyon, there's not a damn thing you can do about it. If you want Keisha, then you need to go after her."

"Damn it, Zane, she doesn't trust me. She believes the worst about me."

"Get over it, or live the rest of your life without her. There's nothing you shouldn't be able to forgive her for, even if it was her losing faith in you. From what I gather, Bonita Simpkins set you up pretty damn good, and I wouldn't give her the satisfaction of knowing her plan worked."

Zane glanced at his watch again. The movie would start in an hour. Channing had said she would be right back, and he couldn't help but wonder what was taking her so long.

"Maybe you're right," Canyon said. "I went to Bonita when it happened and tried to get her to tell Keisha the truth, but she refused."

Zane looked at his watch again. "Look, Canyon, I got to go. I've given you all the advice I'm going to give on this Keisha matter. You're on your own from here on out. Goodbye." He then clicked off the phone.

Moving out of the bedroom, he headed for the front

door. Evidently Channing had gotten into a conversation with Jennifer and forgotten their date. He would just have to go next door and remind her.

Channing walked the beach as she swiped at the tears that couldn't seem to stop flowing. When was she going to stop being a fool? And for the same man!

He had played her well, and what hurt her more than anything else was that there had been no need for him to do that. Why couldn't he just let her go? Why did he have to follow her here with lies, lies and more lies? There was no way he could refute what he'd told Canyon. Words she'd heard with her own ears.

"I'm not falling in love with Channing. I just told her that."

The memory made Channing cry harder, made her chest ache and her head hurt. It seemed she'd been walking the beach for hours when she knew it had only been a few minutes. Clenching her fist in anger, she turned around. It was time to go back and confront Zane, tell him he had played his last game on her …

She gasped when suddenly the sand beneath her feet gave away and she began to sink. "Oh, God!" She tried pulling her feet out, but it only made her sink deeper.

Frantically, she glanced around. It was pitch-dark, and she could barely see the lights from the homes at Kindle Shores. It occurred to her then just how far she had walked. She knew the area. It was one swimmers and sunbathers were warned to avoid for this very reason. Years ago, she had heard how a couple who had been strolling along this particular section of the beach had met their fate when they both went down in quicksand. They had drowned from the high tide before the search party had found them.

Channing willed herself not to panic. She had to try and remain calm. Each time she attempted to pull her feet free, she sank lower. What was she going to do? She didn't have her cell phone with her and hadn't told anyone where she was going. And why had she walked so close to the shoreline?

When she sank lower still, she fought back tears. Would Zane come looking for her? He should be the last person she wanted to see, but right now she would give anything to see his face. He had no idea where she was, but she had to believe he would come.

She had to believe that.

"Channing left here a half hour ago," Jennifer said to Zane. "I was standing on the porch, and I watched her go inside. After that, I came in here to give the kids their baths."

"I saw her go back out," Ronald added, coming to stand beside his wife. "Channing hadn't been inside her house more than a few minutes before she ran back out. I was still outside picking up the kids' toys when I saw her. She was walking quickly down the beach." He hesitated and then added, "She seemed upset about something."

Upset? Zane frowned. *Why would Channing be upset?*

"I wouldn't know why she would be upset," he said. "Maybe she just wanted to take a walk before we went out. We're supposed to be going to the movies."

Jennifer nodded. "She did mention that. That's the reason she said she had to rush back. So it's strange for her to wander off when she seemed so eager to go out with you."

Zane had to agree. That was strange. "Well, thanks.

Hopefully she'll be back soon," he said, glancing down the dark stretch of beach. He couldn't see a thing. The thought of Channing being out there didn't sit well with him. It made him feel uneasy.

"On second thought, I think I'll go look for her," he said, walking off the Farmers' porch.

"Need any help?" Ronald offered.

"No, I'll probably meet her on her way back," Zane said hopefully.

"If you don't, you have my number," Ronald reminded him. "Call me."

"I will," Zane said over his shoulder. Ronald had given Zane his number when Ronald had inquired about the purchase of a pony for his daughter. Zane had promised to check on it when he got back to Denver and give the man a call as to whether Born Free's foal was for sale.

Zane began walking toward the beach, and that uneasy feeling just wouldn't go away. Ronald had said Channing seemed upset, but Zane didn't have a clue as to what could have upset her. Nothing had been awry when she'd left to take the food over to the Farmers. She had even given him a kiss before leaving.

He did recall that not long after she'd left to go next door he had returned Canyon's call. He'd talked to his cousin until right before he'd gone to the Farmers for Channing. That meant she returned during the time he'd been on the phone with Canyon.

Zane searched his mind for why she would have come inside the house only to leave a few moments later. Could she have overheard his conversation with Canyon? If she had, there was nothing said that would have upset her. In fact, he'd given his cousin advice about Keisha again.

Zane stopped walking when he suddenly recalled something. It was when Canyon mentioned him falling in love with Channing. Zane's response had been, *"I'm not falling in love with Channing. I just told her that."*

But then Zane had proceeded to clarify what he'd meant. But what if Channing had heard the first part of his conversation with Canyon and not the second? His guts twisted at the thought that she might be somewhere assuming he was making a fool out of her, assuming he had no intention of falling in love with her. He could see how that would trouble her.

Zane picked up his pace as he looked up and down the shoreline. It was dark, so he pulled out the miniature flashlight on his key chain.

The thought that something had happened to Channing pricked his skin. There was no way he was going to lose her. No way.

Channing tried fighting her fear, but it was useless. From the moon's light, she could see the ocean and it appeared to be coming closer, which meant the high tide had started. The water's spray was hitting her in the face. Already she had sunk down to her waist and was sinking faster by the minute. It was as though the sand was pulling her in.

Once or twice she thought she had heard someone walking around, but when she'd called out no one was there. Was this how her life was to end? She felt tired, drained; she began imagining all kinds of crazy stuff. Didn't her brother once tell her about wild dogs that roamed the beaches at night? Even snakes. And here she was being held captive by the earth.

No! In protest, she tried moving one of her feet and then cried out in frustration when it sank a foot farther into the sand. Then the ocean water began hitting her in the chest.

She knew without being told that the tide was coming closer.

Zane stopped walking and scanned his flashlight ahead of him. Would Channing have come this far? What if she'd taken another path, away from the beach, and was walking through one of the trails to return home? He was about to turn around, hoping that was what she had done, when he heard a faint sound. Automatically he moved toward it and began calling Channing's name.

Channing tried calling out several times. "Help me! Somebody please help me." The sand had covered her up to her breasts, and she was sinking faster.

She went still when she thought she heard her name.

Was she imagining things?

She listened and heard it again. It was Zane's voice. She was sure of it.

"Zane! I'm over here. In quicksand. Please help me!"

A few moments later, she saw a flash of light, and then it was aimed at her. She heard Zane's colorful expletives as he raced toward her.

"No, Zane!" she shouted. "Don't come any closer, or you might get stuck, as well. You need to go get help."

Zane had already assessed the situation. There was no time to get help, but he did pull out his cell phone and call Ronald to tell him to come quick with rope and his truck. Zane glanced around. The tide was coming in, and already the sand had covered Channing nearly to her neck.

He knew he had to keep her calm, but he couldn't just wait for help to arrive. He moved around, tentatively testing the area surrounding her and was glad the quicksand was confined to the little area where she was. That meant he could attempt to pull her out if she held on to him.

"Okay, Channing, listen up, baby. I'm going to need you to arch your body back as far as it will go. That will help spread out your weight and make it harder for you to keep sinking. I'll get behind you on hard sand. Extend your arms back to me, and I'll pull you out while you try working your legs free."

Channing heard Zane's instructions, but the minute she moved her body to arch her back she sank deeper. "Zane!"

Zane tried to stay in control of his emotions, but he was two seconds from jumping in there with her. "Channing, don't rush. Take your time. Arch your back, and extend your arms backward so I can grab them," he said, lying flat on his stomach as close as he could get to her.

"No! I might pull you in and you'll die with me."

"I'd rather die with you than live without you, damn it. You are my life, and I won't lose you. I won't. Now bend your back as far as you can, and extend your arms over your head to me."

He knew he was taking a chance because he would be relying on his strength to pull her out. "Now do it!"

The demand in his voice was sharp. She arched her back, and he could see her struggling. "Don't fight, Channing. Just arch like you're in a pool trying to float on your back."

Channing followed his directions and found spreading her weight was helping. She could even disentangle her legs a little. "My legs are loosening up some," she said with excitement in her voice.

"Arch a little bit more, Channing. We're not there yet. I need to grab your arms. Bring them back over your head as far as you can. Pretend I'm about to make love to you and I need your body shaped like a bow, lifting up off the bed."

He gave a deep sigh when he extended his hands out as far as he could without tumbling into the quicksand with her. He came close to touching her fingertips. "That's it, baby. Arch your back just a little more, and I'll pull you out."

"It hurts," she moaned.

"I know, baby, but do it. Do it for me. I'll die if anything happens to you. I can't lose you."

He sounded almost convincing, Channing thought as she closed her eyes and tried arching her back some more. But she knew the truth about how he felt. Still, she tried moving her legs. "I think I lost my sandal. It was one of my new ones."

"I'll buy you another pair," he said, knowing that she was exhausted. But he couldn't let her give up. The tide was coming in fast. He almost yelled for joy when he was finally able to catch Channing's hands in a tight grip.

Now came the hard part.

Placing all his strength on his shoulders, he closed his eyes and began his attempt to extricate her from the quicksand. A couple of times he almost lost his grip, but he refused to let go.

He pulled with all his might, trying to ignore the pressure on both their arms. He knew he was slowly pulling her free, and when he was able to catch her around her upper chest, he reached out and grabbed tight. That's when the heavy beams of a pickup truck shone on them before coming to a stop. Several men jumped out. Zane didn't take his gaze off Channing, but he knew it was Ronald and he had brought others to help.

Zane felt his grip loosen on Channing and cursed. Ronald and several guys surrounded him with huge flat lumber, which provided a bridgelike surface that let them get closer to Channing. While they held the bridge in place, Zane crawled over it and grabbed her by the waist.

He knew someone had tied a rope around him and was pulling him back, and he was bringing Channing with him. It took great effort, but when she was completely free from the quicksand, the men cheered. He gathered Channing close while she cried in his arms.

Fourteen

Zane sat in a chair beside the bed and watched as Channing slept. He'd held her in his lap in Ronald's truck all the way home. Then he had held her while they showered, washing off enough sand to start their own beach. He'd even washed her hair because she was too tired to do it herself.

Then he had toweled her dry and dressed her in pj's and placed her beneath the covers. That was when the doctor had come, an older man who lived in the community and still made house calls. Dr. Peterson had said the pills he'd given her would make her sleep for a while. Already she'd been sleeping for four hours, and Zane was still here, sitting by her bedside.

He'd never known real fear until tonight. When he thought about how close he'd come to losing her. What if he'd given up searching earlier and turned around? What if he hadn't heard her cry for help? What if he hadn't taken that first-aid training years ago, which had taught him what to do if you become lodged in quicksand? What if—

"Zane?"

He jerked when he heard Channing's voice and was out of the bed in a flash. He moved to sit next to her. "Yes, sweetheart? How do you feel?"

"Like hell."

He nodded in understanding. Dr. Peterson had said she would be sore for a couple of days. She had strained a lot of muscles while arching her back. "Is there anything you need? Water? Juice? Milk? Sorry, you can't have any wine, thanks to the medicine you're taking."

She gently grabbed his wrist and saw the scratches her hands had made trying to hold on to him. "Why, Zane? Why would you risk your life to save mine?"

Zane sighed deeply. Now more than ever he had to make her understand…and believe. "Because I don't have a life without you, Channing. I told you while you were in that quicksand, and I meant it."

She didn't say anything for a minute and then slowly released his hand. "But I heard what you told Canyon, Zane," she said accusingly. "You told him that you were not falling in love with me. That you'd only told me that."

So he'd been right. She had overheard the first part of his conversation with Canyon. "Yes, I told him that."

He saw the crushed look that appeared on her face, and when she made a move to turn her back to him, he said, "But you ran off before overhearing the rest of our conversation, Channing. Had you stuck around, you would have heard me clarify what I meant. The reason I can't fall in love with you is because I'm already in love with you."

He shifted to lie beside her in the bed. He needed to touch her. To hold her.

"I knew when I left Denver to come here that I loved you. And it happened just like I said. But you didn't believe me, Channing. You thought I was confusing love and lust. But I knew how I felt. It was you who had doubt. So I came up with a plan.

"Since you thought I wasn't in love with you, I wanted to let you think I was *falling* in love with you. If you needed to see the transformation, then I had no problem showing it to you. For I am a changed man, Channing. I've never loved any woman before, but I do love you. I want to give you my love. I want to give you my name, and I want to give you my babies."

He eased off the bed and went to the drawer where he'd placed the items he'd taken out of his luggage. He reached inside and pulled out the locked box and carried it over to the bed. "This box holds all my treasures. I purchased it the day after you left town," he said, taking the key out of his pocket.

"This is what kept me going after you left me, Channing. All I had were the memories."

Channing slowly eased up in bed, fighting against the pain of doing so. Her eyes widened when Zane pulled out the calendar she'd given him a few years ago. "You kept that?" she asked, surprised.

"Yes, and it was my lifeline. I would spend hours and hours looking through it and was too stupid to figure out why." He placed the calendar aside and pulled out another item. The gold chain.

Channing gasped again, surprised. "I thought..."

"What did you think, Channing? That I would pawn it? Give it to another woman? I bought it for you and only you," he said, reaching out and placing it around her neck where it belonged. "I didn't want it back, but you insisted. So I kept it in here, and this is where it's been ever since."

He didn't say anything for a long moment. "The last item in here is something you haven't seen before. Something I purchased before leaving Denver to come here. It's something I intended to give you when the time was right. When I knew I had convinced you that I loved you."

He reached inside and pulled out a small white jeweler's box and handed it to her.

Channing held Zane's gaze as she took the box from him. Her heart began beating fast and furious in her chest. She broke eye contact with him to open the lid and then gasped at the beautiful diamond ring.

"Channing, will you marry me? I love you so much, and I don't want to be separated from you for a single night. If I have to move to Atlanta, that's fine. I have family there already. If you and I need to split our time in Denver and Atlanta in an arrangement like Rico and Megan's, then that's fine, too."

Tears Channing couldn't hold back any longer flowed down her cheeks. A misunderstanding had almost cost her her life tonight. Because she hadn't believed Zane's words of love. He'd been saying it, but tonight, in saving her life the way he had, he had shown it.

"So, do you need to think about my proposal?" he asked, breaking into her thoughts.

She swiped at her tears. "No, I don't need to think about it. I love you, and I believe you love me. Tonight you proved just how much."

"I do love you," Zane said, sliding the ring on her finger. "And I want a short engagement."

"I want that, too," she said, smiling as she looked

down at the ring, thinking how beautiful it was. "I'll move from Atlanta to 'Zane's Hideout.' While in Denver, Dr. Rowe, the chief of staff, made me an offer to come back to work at the hospital. I turned her down, but she said she would keep the offer open for six months."

Zane grinned, not believing how nicely things were falling into place. "Riley's getting married in a couple of months, and I don't want to rain on his parade, so what about the month after? That would be in October."

She smiled. "What about a Christmas wedding?"

He let out a deep groan. "The wait will kill me."

She chuckled. "I'll be there to help you manage. If I start the transfer paperwork next week, I can move back to Denver in another month."

"If you did, that would make me a happy man, sweetheart. You have a home already at the Hideout." Conscious of her sore muscles, he shifted his body so he could lower his lips to hers.

He then kissed her with all the love he felt in his heart.

"Then consider it done," she whispered a short while later when he let her come up for air.

And then they sealed their engagement with another kiss.

* * * * *

*Don't miss the next two Westmoreland novels
by Brenda Jackson!*
CANYON
Available August 2013

*Years ago, Canyon Westmoreland let
misunderstandings ruin a good thing. But now
Keisha Ashford has returned—with a two-year-old
son. This time, nothing will stop Canyon from
claiming what is his—his woman and his child!*

STERN
Available September 2013

*When Stern Westmoreland helps his best friend with
a makeover he never expects sizzling attraction to
ignite between them. Now there's only one way to
make her his: have one long, steamy night together as
much more than friends!*

#2245 CANYON
The Westmorelands
Brenda Jackson

When Canyon Westmoreland's ex-lover returns to town, child in tow and needing a safe haven, he's ready to protect what's his, including the son he didn't know he had.

#2246 DEEP IN A TEXAN'S HEART
Texas Cattleman's Club: The Missing Mogul
Sara Orwig

When tradition-bound Texas millionaire Sam Gordon discovers the sexy set designer he shared a passionate night with is pregnant, he proposes. But Lila Hacket won't settle for anything but the real deal— it's true love or bust!

#2247 THE BABY DEAL
Billionaires and Babies
Kat Cantrell

A baby can't be harder than rocket science! But when aerospace billionaire Michael Shaylen inherits a child, he realizes he needs expert help—from the woman who once broke his heart.

#2248 WRONG MAN, RIGHT KISS
Red Garnier

Molly Devaney has been forbidden to Julian Gage his entire life. But when she asks him to help her seduce his brother, Julian must convince her *he's* the man she really wants.

#2249 HIS INSTANT HEIR
Baby Business
Katherine Garbera

When the man who fathered her secret baby comes back to town with plans to take over her family's business, Cari Chandler is suitably shell-shocked. What's a girl to do—especially if the man is irresistible?

#2250 HIS BY DESIGN
Dani Wade

Wedding white meets wedding night when a repressed executive assistant at a design firm finds herself drawn to the unconventional ideas and desires of her new boss.

REQUEST YOUR FREE BOOKS!
2 FREE NOVELS PLUS 2 FREE GIFTS!

ALWAYS POWERFUL, PASSIONATE AND PROVOCATIVE

YES! Please send me 2 FREE Harlequin Desire® novels and my 2 FREE gifts (gifts are worth about $10). After receiving them, if I don't wish to receive any more books, I can return the shipping statement marked "cancel." If I don't cancel, I will receive 6 brand-new novels every month and be billed just $4.55 per book in the U.S. or $4.99 per book in Canada. That's a savings of at least 13% off the cover price! It's quite a bargain! Shipping and handling is just 50¢ per book in the U.S. and 75¢ per book in Canada.* I understand that accepting the 2 free books and gifts places me under no obligation to buy anything. I can always return a shipment and cancel at any time. Even if I never buy another book, the two free books and gifts are mine to keep forever.

225/326 HDN F4ZC

Name _____ (PLEASE PRINT) _____

Address _____ Apt. #

City _____ State/Prov. _____ Zip/Postal Code

Signature (if under 18, a parent or guardian must sign)

Mail to the **Harlequin® Reader Service:**
IN U.S.A.: P.O. Box 1867, Buffalo, NY 14240-1867
IN CANADA: P.O. Box 609, Fort Erie, Ontario L2A 5X3

Want to try two free books from another line?
Call 1-800-873-8635 or visit www.ReaderService.com.

* Terms and prices subject to change without notice. Prices do not include applicable taxes. Sales tax applicable in N.Y. Canadian residents will be charged applicable taxes. Offer not valid in Quebec. This offer is limited to one order per household. Not valid for current subscribers to Harlequin Desire books. All orders subject to credit approval. Credit or debit balances in a customer's account(s) may be offset by any other outstanding balance owed by or to the customer. Please allow 4 to 6 weeks for delivery. Offer available while quantities last.

Your Privacy—The Harlequin® Reader Service is committed to protecting your privacy. Our Privacy Policy is available online at www.ReaderService.com or upon request from the Harlequin Reader Service.

We make a portion of our mailing list available to reputable third parties that offer products we believe may interest you. If you prefer that we not exchange your name with third parties, or if you wish to clarify or modify your communication preferences, please visit us at www.ReaderService.com/consumerchoice or write to us at Harlequin Reader Service Preference Service, P.O. Box 9062, Buffalo, NY 14269. Include your complete name and address.

Canyon watched Keisha turn into Mary's Little Lamb Day Care. He frowned. Why would she be stopping at a day care? Maybe she had volunteered to babysit for someone tonight.

He slid into a parking spot and watched as she got out of her car and went inside, smiling. Hopefully, her good mood would continue when she saw that he'd followed her. His focus stayed on her, concentrating on the sway of her hips with every step she took, until she was no longer in sight. A few minutes later she walked out of the building, smiling and chatting with the little boy whose hand she was holding—a boy who was probably around two years old.

Canyon studied the little boy's features. The kid could be a double for Denver, Canyon's three-year-old nephew. An uneasy feeling stirred his insides. Then, as he studied the little boy, Canyon took in a gasping breath. There was only one reason the little boy looked so much like a Westmoreland.

Canyon gripped the steering wheel, certain steam was coming out of his ears.

He didn't remember easing his seat back, unbuckling his

seat belt or opening the car door. Neither did he remember walking toward Keisha. However, he would always remember the look on her face when she saw him. What he saw on her features was surprise, guilt and remorse.

As he got closer, defensiveness followed by fierce protectiveness replaced those other emotions. She pulled her son—the child he was certain was *their* son—closer to her side. "What are you doing here, Canyon?"

He came to a stop in front of her. His body was radiating anger from the inside out. His gaze left her face to look down at the little boy, who was clutching the hem of Keisha's skirt and staring up at him with distrustful eyes.

Canyon shifted his gaze back up to meet Keisha's eyes. In a voice shaking with fury, he asked, "Would you like to tell me why I didn't know I had a son?"

CANYON
by New York Times *and* USA TODAY *bestselling author*
Brenda Jackson
Available August 2013
only from Harlequin® Desire®!

Love the Harlequin book you just read?

Your opinion matters.

Review this book on your favorite
book site, review site, blog or your own
social media properties and share
your opinion with other readers!

SADDLE UP AND READ 'EM!

Looking for another great Western read? Check out these August reads from the PASSION category!

CANYON by Brenda Jackson
The Westmorelands
Harlequin Desire

THE HEART WON'T LIE by Vicki Lewis Thompson
Sons of Chance
Harlequin Blaze

Look for these great Western reads AND MORE available wherever books are sold or visit
www.Harlequin.com/Westerns

Kick back and relax with a

HARLEQUIN®

Desire

book

Passion, wealth and drama make these books a must-have for those so-so days. The perfect combination when paired with a comfy chair and your favorite drink or on the subway with your morning coffee. Plunge into a world of **hot cowboys, sexy alpha-heroes,** secret pregnancies, family sagas and **passionate love stories.** Each book is sure to fulfill your fantasies and leave you wanting more.

HARLEQUIN®
entertain, enrich, inspire™